The
Freedom of Innocence

A JOURNEY INTO THE HEART OF ALL THAT IS

Lara A. Shah

For information, please contact Aquarian Age Publishing, Inc., 102 NE 2nd Street, #141, Boca Raton, FL. 33432

ISBN-10: 0-9767530-0-6
ISBN-13: 978-0-9767530-0-1

LCCN: 2005903199

Aquarian Age Publishing, Inc.

www.aquarianagepublishing.com

This book is affectionately
dedicated to
The 13 Infinite Stars of Light.

My gratitude goes beyond words.

Acknowledgments

Even though it seemed to me at times that this book was the result of my blood, sweat and tears alone, that was only an appearance . . . the truth of the matter is that this little book was a big team effort. Much of the team is of the "invisible" kind. There are a few though, actually in a body, who have made invaluable contributions one way or another. Two very special people that I hold the highest regard for—Jacqueline Muller, my dear soul sister, played an essential role during my "remembering" process. She was not made into a character in this fictional story, but she was certainly part of the real story. And Helen Barton, whose input and wisdom on the Universal Laws helped me to gain a much deeper understanding of how the Divine Laws of Healing are operating. Thank you, both. And heartfelt thanks to another soul sister, Diane Wilcoxson, for reminding me that "play" is what it is all about.

As far as publishing logistics are concerned, I must acknowledge Sylvia Hemmerly of Publishing Professionals for doing the interior design and answering about a half a million questions; a guru in the industry and a God-send for me. Also, Karen Saunders of

Macgraphics Services (along with Joyce M. Turley) for a cover design that's actually in harmony with the Divine Laws I have written about…wow!, and Barbara McNichol for doing a great job editing all my gibberish. Last but not least, thanks to Adam Wyde for helping out with my illustrations.

In a gesture of palms together at the heart, I would like to honor all the individuals who have crossed my path and blessed my life . . . some with their love, others with their judgment.

All of it was, and is, just perfect . . . and I thank you.

–Lara

Contents

Author's Note

The following is a fictional tale with fictional characters. As with many works of fiction though, this one is partially based on my own life experiences.

This travelogue-style tale provides an introduction to the 12 Divine Laws of Healing. In reality, each Law is so intricately detailed, that I have decided not to include those details in this first book. Neither was I patient enough to sit and write too much nor do I claim to have even comprehended all that these Divine Laws encompass. The second book, however, is already in the making!

So, through this parable, I aim to capture the basic essence of these 12 Laws, and present them in a way that's easy to understand and enjoyable to read. They were neither channeled nor learned. Rather, they were *remembered* during the course of two particularly transformative years of my life.

A lot of metaphor and symbolism has been intentionally used throughout this narrative. It may not be obvious, so I thought I'd just mention it here at the beginning.

When I write "All That Is," I am referring to what many prefer to call "God"; others prefer to call "Supreme Being," and so on. To me, it is the same.

It is my greatest joy to now share my truth with you. May it touch your soul.

"I would not interfere with any creed of yours, nor want to appear that I have all the cures. There is so much to know, so many things are true. The way my feet must go may not be the best for you. So I give this spark of what is light to me, to guide you through the dark but not tell you what to see."

—Anonymous

With love and grace from the heart of All That Is,

Lara

What is the Journey of the Human Soul but a Journey Back to Innocence. . . .

"Once spirit comes down to dwell in the flesh it starts to create what is called a soul, for soul is that part of our being which is built up through experiences undergone by the tender inner self during incarnation. Soul can further be described as the feminine aspect of human life, the mother principle. The soul of the world is made up of the feeling of the world.

In esoteric teaching you will always find the soul referred to as representing the mother or feminine aspect of life, the second principle—the first principle being divine will, the father or masculine aspect.

Soul gives feeling to the self and is the intuitive part of every being. The Age of Aquarius will bring the mother or woman aspect of life into greater prominence. In other words, it will usher in greater development of intuition. . . ."

"The Living Word of St. John—
White Eagle's Interpretation of the Gospel"
By: White Eagle. Third Edition (Revised)
The White Eagle Publishing Trust 1949, 1979, 2000
Excerpt from the first chapter, 'Soul and Spirit'.

The Journey Commences. . . .

ANANYA WAS BORN A WORLD TRAVELER, and by the time she reached 35 years of age, she had already lived in seven different countries across the globe. She belonged everywhere and nowhere at the same time, and she felt comfortable with that. She had journeyed far, and not just geographically. Ananya, like so many others in today's world, had passed through her share of trials and tribulations growing up in a "dysfunctional" family.

Both curious and deeply contemplative, she sought to understand everything, because it was in the understanding that she felt a part of things.

Ananya was an independent, courageous, and free spirited individual. When something called to her heart, she heeded without much hesitation. Through experience, she was discovering that all the answers to every question resided in one's own heart.

In recent years, Ananya had been learning—sometimes the hard way—to listen to and follow her heart, and not her mind. And in so doing, she was finally allowing the destiny of her soul to unfold.

In the past, when she allowed her personality to rule—what her *ego* thought would give her happiness—things never quite worked out. It was only when she began to tune into her heart center and listen to its wisdom, that she discovered where happiness and fulfillment lie— within.

By listening to her heart, she now found herself far away from her South Florida base—in Cairo, Egypt.

* * *

Her adventure started with a vivid dream in which she saw the 12 Pyramids of Giza. In this dream the Pyramids were alive and had a message to convey. She kept hearing her name and hearing that the time was finally right in the history of humanity for the truth of these Pyramids to be known again.

Ananya awoke from that dream in a daze, as if her spirit were not fully in her body. She lay in the bed for a while, thinking. It really didn't feel like a dream at all . . . it felt too real, more real, even, than what she could see in her own bedroom at that moment.

She heard her name being called again, followed by the words: **"Custodian of the Divine Laws of Healing."** She checked to see if she was still sleeping . . . her eyes were open . . . the clock on the nightstand read 9:22 a.m. *"I guess I'm late for work,"* she thought, then rolled over and dug her head into her favorite goose-down pillow. Another thought ran through her head. *"Okay, so it's confirmed I'm not sleeping, not dreaming . . . I'm awake. I'm awake, and I'm hearing things . . . great."* Although she didn't really understand what it was all about, she knew it was significant because her entire body was buzzing with energy.

What started out as a gentle whisper saying her name gradually grew into sort of a scream . . . not an angry scream, but a loud one. She felt a clear and intense conviction that her heart simply could not deny or ignore. She knew she needed to go to the Pyramids of Giza; something called her there for some reason.

Her logical mind was quite perplexed at how these ancient structures were going to convey their message. She also had a funny feeling in her stomach that she would be in many other places, too. This would not be a quick trip. Not yet understanding why, where or how long, she was still willing to accept the adventure. Thankful she had flexibility as a freelance writer; she packed her laptop and traveled to Egypt without delay.

* * *

Arrangements had been made for Ananya to be picked up from the hotel in downtown Cairo and driven to Giza. She had been to Egypt before and seen the Pyramids, but she was about to find out that she had not actually *seen* the Pyramids.

Although the wind was blowing sand in every direction, Ananya was grateful for its movement because it gave some reprieve from the blistering heat. She looked for a relatively private spot—hard to come by in Giza with all the camel drivers harassing visitors to buy camel rides. She sat down on a rock with all the Pyramids in view. Within a moment she was no longer looking at the Pyramids; instead, they were being *shown* to her.

What Ananya was shown were these 12 Pyramids in all their original, ancient glory, each one in brilliant color with the most immaculate artwork displayed both inside and out. It was the most spectacular thing she had ever seen. Strangely, she recognized this artwork as if it were her own. All together, the colorful paintings seemed to convey a story, with each pyramid telling its own chapter of that story.

As she sat, Ananya became aware of being contained within something. She looked up to the sky and all around until she could actually see the form of another pyramid, which was obviously invisible to most people because it wasn't in the form of dense matter like the others. This "ethereal" pyramid was so vast that it covered all the 12 visible pyramids and beyond.

Just like in her dream, it seemed that these ancient structures were somehow "alive." *"Is that even possible?"* she thought. And at that moment her thought was answered with a gentle voice coming from the direction of the Pyramids, saying *"It is."*

Overcome with amazement and awe, Ananya was barely aware of the camel driver pestering her to take a camel ride. At the same time, a feeling of sadness overwhelmed her. Here she was, being shown the reality of what these Pyramids once were: magnificent *living* energies, and yet today all people tend to see is the colorless stone. But now *she* knew that these structures were indeed alive, and if they were alive, then they could and would communicate somehow. She would open herself up to the *possibility* of that happening. So she took a deep breath and silently invited these living beings to communicate with her, just as they had done in her dream.

A voice spoke in her head, very clearly and with loving authority. *"We are a physical manifestation of the Divine Laws of the Universe. The artwork on our walls is a most ancient and sacred text, and within the pages lie all the secrets of the universe."*

She was then shown the image of a color spectrum, which appeared in the air in front of her. A voice said, *"White is the sum of all the colors, just as love is the sum of all emotions. There is one Law that is the sum of all the other Laws. This one big Law is represented by the one big 'invisible' Pyramid. Just like the Pyramids, all the other Laws are actually contained within this one big Law."*

With a deep sense of wonder, Ananya realized she had connected telepathically with the energy of these Pyramids, so she asked questions in the form of thoughts about the information she was being given.

"What are these Laws of the Universe?"

"The Divine Laws by which existence itself operates. There are 12 Divine Laws and of these 12, four of them are what you might call primary laws, similar to the existence of primary colors on the color spectrum."

She felt waves of energy running through her—as if something that had been dormant for many lifetimes became suddenly activated again.

"You have seen our original state of being, how glorious we once were. It has been well over 10,000 years of your earth time since then," the voice continued.

"And. . . . what is the reason for the sadness I feel here? I feel that it is actually your sadness that I am picking up . . . can that be?"

"Yes. It is because mankind has, for the past 10,000 years, made the Divine Laws a limitation, instead of a means of personal expansion. Now, that is not a criticism or a judgment, simply an observation of all the dis-ease in your world today. This is what has erased our brilliant colors, not erosion."

"How can we address all the dis-ease today?"

"To address dis-ease, which is basically an imbalance present in one's understanding of existence; the 12 Divine Laws of Healing may be applied. Each of the 12 Laws of Healing offers a bridge to the 12 Laws of the Universe, and is contained within the Universal Laws. This is important because the Divine Laws of Healing are not a separate set of Laws but a part of the Universal Laws. In fact, one might say that they form the heart of the Universal Laws."

"So, if they are the heart, it seems that if one truly understood the totality of the Universal Laws, then one would automatically understand the Laws of Healing, since the latter is contained within the former. Is that true?"

"Yes, that is true. However—and there is a however—no one in your world, until this point in time, has understood the totality of the Universal Laws. In fact, there are great gaps in the current understanding of the Universal Laws, which is why it is crucial to approach them from the perspective of the Divine Laws of Healing. The Laws of Healing will provide the necessary bridge over those gaps. It is akin to learning how to walk before one can run—and every human baby first walked before they gained the proper understanding about how to run."

"And why are they called the Laws of Healing?"

"Have you considered what healing is? Healing is everything. It entails not only being open to All That Is, but also an openness to being a part of All That Is. Healing is about viewing the world with love, not fear. The moment there is fear, innocence is lost and dis-ease is created. Do you see?"

"Yes . . . I . . . um. . . . "

"The Laws of Healing address the imbalances, the dis-ease caused by the misunderstanding or misapplication of the Universal Laws. So, it is this set of Laws, the Divine Laws of Healing, which need to be re-addressed in your world at this time. We say re-addressed because these Laws have always been in your world; they have just been forgotten. It is time to remember. And that is why you are here."

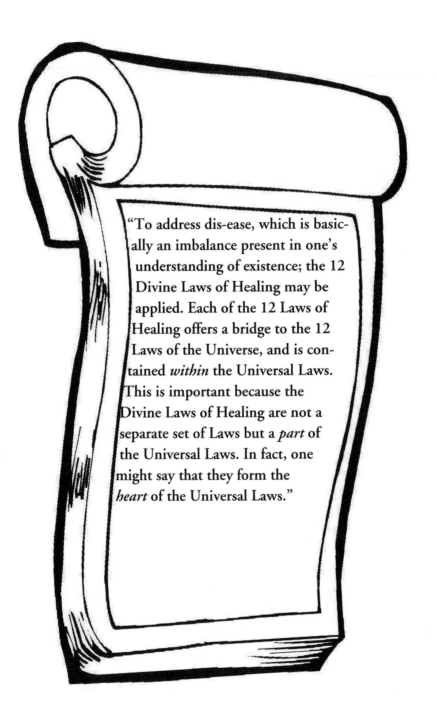

"To address dis-ease, which is basically an imbalance present in one's
understanding of existence; the 12
Divine Laws of Healing may be
applied. Each of the 12 Laws of
Healing offers a bridge to the 12
Laws of the Universe, and is contained *within* the Universal Laws.
This is important because the
Divine Laws of Healing are not a
separate set of Laws but a *part* of
the Universal Laws. In fact, one
might say that they form the
heart of the Universal Laws."

Ananya sat glued to the rock she was sitting on. *"Me?"* she thought to herself, *"Are they sure they haven't mixed me up with someone else?"*

She was silent for awhile, eyes fixated on the ground below her feet. *"And . . . once these Divine Laws of Healing are rediscovered, then what?"* she asked, looking up and suddenly feeling as humble as a speck of dust.

"If they are activated within the souls of the people in your world, then those souls will, if they choose, ascend to higher and higher dimensions of being. Dimensions where there is no dis-ease of any kind."

With overwhelming waves of energy still coursing through her body, it suddenly hit her: The Pyramids of Giza were not ancient tombs for dead Egyptian kings. She never believed that theory anyway, but now she understood. These 12 Pyramids each housed one Universal Law and one Divine Law of Healing! She wished she had a loud speaker so she could announce this to everyone there.

"Those were the chapters I was seeing, chapters of a most beautiful journey—the journey of the human soul."

The voice became unbelievably tender for a moment. . . . *"That is so, little one."*

"Little one!?" she thought in utter bewilderment. That's a term of endearment—referring to her petite stature—that only her closest friends used.

"Now, please understand that the Universal Laws and the Divine Laws of Healing do not operate in the same way civil law operates in your world. These Laws

are not something to obey, but living energies to explore and experience. These Laws do not contain condemnation, criticism, or judgment. They are, very simply, all about freedom."

"What kind of freedom?"

"True freedom; inner freedom. It is the sense of completeness, fulfillment, and joy within."

"It's the kind of freedom that no one can take away from you."

"That is so. Understanding these Laws, and how they operate, is beneficial because if one flows in harmony with their energy, one can know bliss."

"Well, bliss sounds good to me!"

"You see, everyone is always living these Laws, whether one is aware of it or not. The universe is based on them; they are constantly operating. So, the secret to an existence of ease, grace, and joy lies in flowing with and embracing what is. If, however, one decides not to flow with the energy of the Laws, one is not going to get punished for it. In fact, one's resistance to these Laws is actually part of one's experience of them. Therefore, it is not possible to do anything 'wrong', you see. People often forget that they are actually spiritual beings, here on earth to have a human experience . . . not the other way around. From that perspective, as spiritual beings, you are already perfect. And so everything you do on earth is just an exploration of that perfection. Granted, there are a variety of ways in which to explore, and so each situation in life is perfect as it is—for that moment."

This new perspective created such a feeling of empowerment within Ananya, she didn't care that she was getting sun burnt and covered with sand by this point. It would take time to digest it all, but one small detail left her puzzled. *"You say there are 12 Divine Laws and I am being shown 13 pyramids. If each pyramid houses one law, then . . . "*

"Then what does that tell you?"

"Well, I guess that tells me that one of the pyramids isn't housing a law; perhaps it's representing something else."

"You are very clever indeed."

She waited for more than this simple confirmation, but she only heard silence, as if that was all that needed to be communicated for the moment. She got the impression that the rest was for her to discover on her own.

Although Ananya never wore a watch, she sensed her driver had been waiting for her long enough. It was time to go, so she asked these great beings who had been communicating with her for permission to leave. They responded with, *"Henceforth, we will be walking beside you."*

* * *

On the long car ride back to the hotel, Ananya closed her eyes and tried to integrate all that she had just experienced. She recalled their last words. *"Are they still really with me?"* she wondered. Just then, she felt a warm buzzing sensation around her heart and heard the words, *"We are here."*

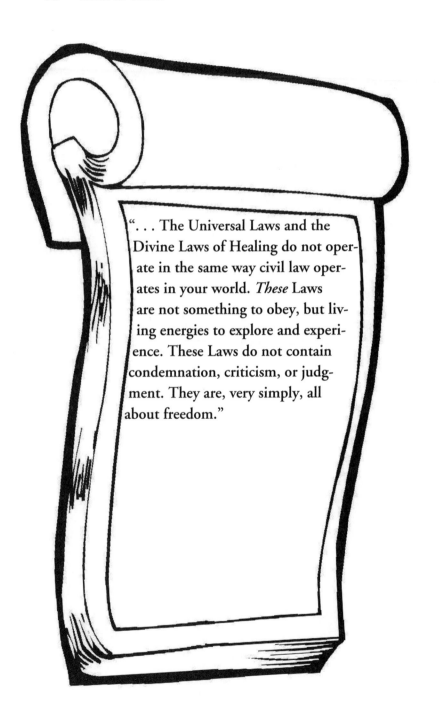

". . . The Universal Laws and the Divine Laws of Healing do not operate in the same way civil law operates in your world. *These* Laws are not something to obey, but living energies to explore and experience. These Laws do not contain condemnation, criticism, or judgment. They are, very simply, all about freedom."

A tear jumped out of her eye. She briefly struggled with her logical mind, which told her all this was simply her imagination. But even her mind knew what it took to make this tough woman cry. Not one who expressed emotions with ease, Ananya's tear let her know that she was not imagining anything.

Keeping her hand on her heart, she asked, *"How will I learn these Divine Laws of Healing?"* The answer came from the depths of her being.

"You do not need to learn them, they are already within you. You will simply remember them."

"How is that?" she inquired with shock. *"I'm going to remember them?"*

"You will. You will because you are a custodian of these Laws . . . they are embedded within you."

Her body began to shake. It felt as if every one of her cells was now waking up, though she had no idea they had even been asleep. Was she really a keeper of these ancient Laws? Was she indeed carrying the knowledge of these Divine Laws of Healing somewhere deep down inside? More immediately, was the driver aware that his passenger was shaking in the back seat? She heard the voice again.

"The Divine Laws of Healing are indeed embedded deeply within your being. And you, though you are not consciously aware of it, have been waiting for the appropriate time to bring them forth. We are here to remind you of this, to let you know that the time has come, and to assist you in remembering. Go on with your journeying; that

must occur. You already knew that you would be going on a long journey, did you not?"

"Yes, yes I did. . . . " and she *had* known it from that funny feeling in her stomach.

"And you will know exactly where you need to go. Actually, it does not matter where you journey to, because it is the process of the journeying itself that will open you to that which is already within your being. The key is in the journey itself. Be assured, we walk beside you."

Ananya let her thoughts drift to her next move. She had a few more days in Egypt, after which she wouldn't be going home. Like they said, she would know exactly where to go and, for some reason, she was feeling drawn to countries she had previously lived in. Remembering the Divine Laws of Healing wasn't a matter of discovering something new, but reconnecting with something old—ancient in fact—so Ananya would journey to her old, familiar places.

From Egypt, she decided she would go north to Turkey, and from there she would set out on an eastward trek to India, Thailand, Japan, and then south to New Zealand. She would tell her editor that she would remain away for a few months, and then make arrangements for a plane ticket to Istanbul, Turkey. Just like that.

1

The Law of Creation

FOR HER LAST DAY IN EGYPT, Ananya flew down to Abu Simbel in the southern part of the country. As in most sacred sites visited today, the opportunity for profit is never missed, not even in the middle of the desert. Before the temple entrances were a hodge-podge of shops, and whether one fancied a Coca-cola or a fake lapis lazuli statue, it could be found. The sellers made a huge effort to sound genuine; "My friend, special price only for you!" But Ananya kept walking, without distraction, toward the temple complex.

Of the two temples at Abu Simbel, Ananya was drawn to the smaller, less ominous-looking one. It seemed visitors were so awed by the main temple and its larger-than-life statues, that the smaller one was void of crowds. That allowed Ananya to experience the energy of this temple in quiet.

As she entered, her feet led her into a dark corner where cows had been carved into the wall and ceiling centuries ago. She recognized them as representations of Hathor, the Egyptian Goddess who was commonly depicted as a cow, the symbol for fertility and birth, or rebirth.

Although Ananya was alone in this dark little corner of the temple, she felt a force present with her that was so powerful it nearly knocked her over. Stunned, she took a few deep breaths. A warm humming vibration rose quickly from her belly to her heart, until it reached her head. Before she could analyze the sensation in her body, she heard a husky masculine voice speaking in her head. After her experience at the Pyramids earlier, she felt comfortable with this situation, although she was still not used to it!

"The 1st Law of the Universe is the Law of Being, which states that everything simply IS. It is the one umbrella Law that governs all the other Laws. If everything IS, then the purpose of existence lies not in doing, but simply in BEing. Soon you will understand that it is not what you do, but what you BE that matters. You've not quite got it yet, but by the end of your journey you will."

This strong vibration was making Ananya's head hurt, yet she knew she had to remain with it. She hadn't yet grasped the Law of Being. The voice continued to speak.

"You have not incarnated on earth as a human doing, but as a human being, therefore you are essentially here on earth to explore and experience that BEing-ness. It is important to understand that one's personality, one's nature, is not who one BE. Dis-ease occurs when people attach to or

identify with their personality rather than just experiencing it for what it is. That is enough information for you to remember the Law of Healing which addresses The Law of Being. Remember, we walk beside you."

In an instant, Ananya felt the powerful presence leave just as quickly as it had come in. She collapsed gently to the floor. She now realized she had been perspiring profusely despite the coolness of the temple.

Not coincidentally, the smaller temple now began to draw a crowd of tourists. Ananya decided to find a shady spot outside under a tree where she could relax for a while. While she sat, protected under the branches, she reflected on how trees were truly enlightened beings. The trunk of a tree stands firm and steadfast, but when a storm comes, its branches stay flexible. They don't resist the wind. Instead, the branches flow *with* the wind. A tree always moves according to the energy present, while always remaining a tree. Inspired, she recognized that trees, unlike humans, have mastered BEing.

She took out a pen and paper from her bag and quickly scribbled down her thought flow.

In the three-dimensional, linear reality in which we exist on earth, past and future appear to be separate from the present when, in fact, all exists in an eternal now. When we step out of our BEing, out of our eternal now, we easily get stuck in the linear illusion of past and future. We get stuck in the stories we tell ourselves about that past and about that future, stories that actually create our eternal now—a now based on who we believe we are rather than who we truly are.

Ananya didn't know where all this was coming from but she continued to write.

The tendency of so many of us is to manufacture a story about who we think we are, and then allow that story to rule our existence—as opposed to allowing our existence to rule the stories. In some cases, we attach to and identify with our stories so much that we continually repeat and relive them lifetime after lifetime. Ironically, the search for identity becomes the surest way to hold back our spiritual evolvement.

This was beautifully symbolized in the story of Adam and the forbidden apple. Man had a burning desire to define himself, to have an identity separate from the universal ONE, and so he "ate fruit" from the tree of the knowledge of good and evil in order to define himself. This tree could have also been called the tree of judgment. When Adam stepped out of BEing into the world of judgment, he lost the freedom of innocence and took on the limitation of perception and belief..

She put down her pen for a moment and took a few sips from the water bottle in her bag. Not addressing anyone in particular, she asked to be given some examples of attaching to a story and stepping out of BEing.

An example was immediately given in the form of an inspirational thought in her head. Alcoholics going through a 12-step program continually step out of BEing every time they proclaim, "I am an alcoholic." The "I am" *is* who one BE, and anything added to "I am" is a step out of that BEing. "I am an alcoholic" is attaching one's BEing to a story—the story of alcoholism—and thereby placing condition and limitation on the BEing. The individual could say "I am . . . .and I *experience* an addiction to alcohol." This frees the individual to then BE absolutely *anything* that he or she desires to BE.

Another example was given in the same way. Some people proclaim, "I am depressed." But depressed is not who they BE. They are simply spiritual beings *experiencing* the human feeling of depression. There is a world of difference between the two. One is a world of limitation, the other a world of freedom. Life is a self-fulfilling prophecy that has no limitations—except for those we believe in.

So, the answer to the question "Who am I?" is simply "I am," and the answer to the question "What am I doing here?" is simply "To BE who I am."

Ananya then had to think about the story she had attached to, which was a story of sexual abuse. The abuse she experienced as a child led to her believing that she was unacceptable, unworthy, and unappreciated as a woman. This self-limiting belief flavored everything she created in her life. She would get into a relationship with a man, for instance, and then—like an airplane on automatic pilot— would react to her partner from the point of view of her story, rather than responding from her BEing. The relationship would end, but the dis-ease within her remained.

When we are stuck in our stories, in our self-limiting beliefs, we will repeat the same pattern over and over, in the same vicious cycle, until we are able to detach ourselves from our experiences and recreate our beliefs.

Ananya continued to write again, as fast as her pen would allow. . . .

We are constantly creating ourselves and our lives with every single thought and belief. If, for example, one maintains a belief that carbohydrates are a "bad" thing to eat, then one creates the reality of the carbohydrates having a negative effect in the body. On the other hand, if one ate those same carbohydrates without any judgment, without deeming them "bad," the negative affect on the body would simply not occur. A chocolate cake could nourish you if you believed that it would because our body listens to everything we tell it and faithfully accepts whatever it hears.

A single thought that's put into words, which then becomes a belief, is powerful beyond measure. It's powerful because it's *creative*. A scripture came to mind. *"In the beginning was the word, and the word was with God and the word was God"* (John 1:1) . . . and the word bore creation.

"That's it!" she said out loud "Creation!" Ananya recognized that personality *repeats*, while BEing *creates*. The Law of Healing, which bridges the gap to the Law of Being, is about this unlimited creative power innate in All That Is. It's the divine creative energy inherent in all living things that can be applied to step back into one's BEing.

The Law of Creation is the 1st Law of Healing that addresses the Universal Law of Being. It is the umbrella Law that governs All That Is. All That Is is constantly creating and recreating itself.

Ananya then acknowledged that we are *already* the creators of our own life situations, so the point is to become aware of this fact, of the power of creation that lies within. Each adventure that is called to the self, by the self, is so that one might create and recreate, and thus further explore and experience who one BE.

With this, Ananya realized that everything she had ever experienced in life, including her relationships, were merely explorations of who she is. She created those experiences to understand herself better, which explains why there are no coincidences or accidents in life. So, actually, *nothing* she had done or experienced had ever been a waste. From this perspective, there was nothing to ever regret.

"If the entire purpose of existence is to create and recreate who we BE," she thought to herself, *"Then all we're doing on this planet is having an adventure with ourselves. It's one hell of an adventure I've been having with myself!"* she thought, rolling her eyes.

Ananya, wanting confirmation of these thoughts, called on the powerful presence that had been with her in the temple. She instantly felt the humming vibration again, this time just around her heart center.

"So the Law of Creation is the first Divine Law of Healing?"

"That is so. This is one of the primary laws. The Law of Creation states that everything lies within you. All of creation lies within you. Creative power is one's own. This means that you are indeed creating yourself, creating who

you wish to BE, all the time. Remember, just because one has not discovered one's creative power yet, does not deny its existence." With that, the humming ceased, allowing Ananya to sit calmly and BE for a few minutes.

* * *

Ananya realized she soon needed to catch her flight back to Cairo. Slowly making her way out of the sacred site, she became aware of every step she took. She fully recognized that she was creating herself and the reality around her with every single step. What a shift! She felt incredibly empowered, sensing that her old, limiting beliefs about herself, and about existence itself, were gradually fading into abyss.

Ananya barely slept that night. She was still in awe of how the Pyramids called her to Egypt, how "they" were communicating with her, how she had actually remembered the 1st Law of Healing just like they said she would. As she stared at the ceiling from her hotel bed, more insights emerged, as if someone was quietly whispering in her ear.

"The self-limiting beliefs, judgments, and fears are so deeply suppressed in some cases that this internal conflict is externalized as a method of dealing with it. It begins with judging and blaming another individual, and then a whole community, and on a massive scale, with entire nations. This is what truly lies behind war among nations . . . and within nations," she realized.

As Ananya reached for the lamp to find her pen and paper again, she had the insight that war is, essentially, a massive resistance to the Law of Creation. However, like the great beings had stated, *"These Laws are not something to be obeyed. They are simply to be explored and experienced in a variety of ways. And one's resistance to the Laws is part of one's experience of them."* So from this perspective, she pondered, even something as terrible as war had some divine purpose. Even though she would always be an advocate for peace, this put current events in a whole new light.

. . . we are *already* the creators of our own life situations, so the point is to become aware of this fact, of the power of creation that lies within. Each adventure that is called to the self, by the self, is so that one might create and recreate, and thus further explore and experience who one BE.

2

The Law of Love

WHILE WAITING FOR HER FLIGHT to board, Ananya felt wobbly. She sensed she was already a different person from when she first arrived in Egypt. With this sense came the knowledge that she had only just begun and couldn't yet even imagine what was in store for her in the coming days and weeks.

To ground her energy, she walked around glancing at the airport shops where tourists bargained for last-minute souvenirs. A painting on papyrus paper of a beautiful winged goddess caught her eye. The Goddess wore a single feather on her head, reminding Ananya of herself when she had lived for a brief period in Peru. During that time, one of the Shamans she had been writing about gave her a condor feather, which carried healing energy within it. The moment she held it, she could feel its power. Almost instinctively, she placed that feather in her long hair, in the exact same manner that this beautiful Goddess wore her plume. She listened as the shop owner explained that Ananya was looking at a depiction of Ma'at, Goddess of Truth and Justice. Something in her so resonated with the energy of this Goddess that Ananya decided Ma'at must accompany her on her journey. She bought the painting.

Having time to spare, Ananya found a seat in the boarding area. She ever-so-carefully placed her new piece of papyrus into the empty front pocket of her carry-on luggage. Just as she was doing that, a man hurriedly walked by and knocked Ananya's bag onto the floor, slightly crushing the piece of papyrus. This man didn't even notice what he'd done. This infuriated Ananya, but instead of confronting him, she just watched him as he scurried toward the gate. Dressed in grubby clothes and, due to his behavior just a minute ago, she concluded that she didn't have any interest in dealing with him anyway.

* * *

After boarding the plane, Ananya sat in her seat and closed her eyes. She felt that humming vibration in her heart center again and a voice lovingly communicated as if it were a thought in her head.

"The 2nd Law of the Universe is the Law of Love. Universal love is a completely unconditional love. This Law states that it is this love, this absolutely unconditional love, which is the true essence of every single living creature in your world. However, many individuals today have lost a sense of humility. And when humility gets lost,

unconditional love is forgotten. Once these individuals re-member who they BE, they will again feel this frequency of unconditional love, which is the essence of their BEing, of all of our BEing-ness. It is the essence of All That Is."

"So, the key to remembering that we are love lies in having humility?" she asked silently.

"In a way, yes . . . and that is where the 2nd Law of Healing will apply. This 2nd Law is another one of the primary laws. Remember, we walk beside you."

At that moment, she opened her eyes to see that clumsy man who kicked her bag boarding the plane . . . and wouldn't you know it, his seat was right next to hers. Ananya acknowledged that the great beings that were walking beside her had a quirky sense of humor. She gave thanks that at least this was not a long flight.

"How interesting that whenever people have an issue about something, the universe makes sure they're given ample opportunity to deal with it," she thought. The universe made doubly sure this time because the man started chatting with her.

Ananya tried to ignore him, but to no avail. She finally gave up and looked up into the man's eyes—and there it was. In his eyes, she saw his soul. At that moment, she remembered that the 2nd Law of Healing, like the 2nd Law of the Universe, is also the Law of Love. The key of this Law is a simple willingness to be vulnerable; that is what humility is all about.

She would soon learn that one's true strength and power lie in one's willingness to be vulnerable. Like quick flashes, she recalled the many times she had put a protective wall up between herself and others because she feared being hurt and judged by them. But she'd really been hiding, not only from others, but more importantly from herself. She realized the conundrum: *"How is it possible to step into the truth of who one BE when one is hiding from one's self?"*

Yes, Ananya had judged this man, but when she encountered his soul in that instant, all she could see was love —that essence of unconditional love that is inherent in All That Is.

She now understood that this man was acting as a mirror for her, just as we *all* do for each other *all* the time. She conceded that the only way it's possible to recognize qualities, positive or negative, in someone or something else is by possessing those qualities within oneself. Otherwise, how could they be recognized and understood? In judging this man, Ananya was judging aspects of herself that she had not fully accepted and embraced. The part of her that didn't feel "good enough" was acting out of fear.

She then realized that total self-acceptance ends all fear and judgment. *"The more we accept ourselves,"* she thought, *"the more creative we are."* Deeper self-acceptance leads to more clarity within, and more clarity within makes it easier for the creative power to flow through. The consequence of *total* self-acceptance is profound healing on all levels of one's being.

From now on, Ananya resolved, whenever she caught herself being judgmental about another person, she would step back and observe her own self through the eyes of unconditional love and with the intention to see which part of her was calling to be healed. And by acknowledging and accepting that it was about *her*—not the other—she'd transmute her judgment into unconditional love for the other person.

Ananya suddenly saw past this man's grubby clothes and inconsiderate behavior, and felt the spark of God that *is* this person. It didn't mean that she condoned his behavior in the terminal. The Law of Love did *not* call for anyone to be a doormat, allowing people to walk all over others doing whatever they please. That's ridiculous. But to see this man, to see everyone through divine eyes, is what this 2nd Law of Healing calls for.

Ananya found the courage to be vulnerable and proceeded to do something she had never done before. She shared—honestly—with this total stranger, every thought that had been going through her head while maintaining total eye contact with his soul; A liberating experience for both of them.

Ananya felt his gentle hand reach for hers—a pleasant surprise. "Thank you," he said, "Despite what you thought of me, I felt so much warmth and love coming from your heart just now. More than I've felt from anyone in a very long time."

She, too, felt as if chains shackled to her for so long were removed. She was free—free to give and receive love to and from anyone, without judgment.

Her green eyes sparkled. This man that she had dismissed about an hour before had turned into one of the most beautiful human beings she had ever met. Had she held on to her ego, she perhaps would never have discovered this precious soul sitting next to her.

The two, now feeling their inter-connectedness, decided not to say goodbye when they landed in Istanbul. After collecting their luggage, they hopped into a taxi and headed for Üsküdar, on the Anatolian side of the city. Ananya had offered to give her new friend a proper introduction to this city she knew so well, starting with a view of the stunning Bosphorus at sunset.

* * *

From the top of a hill, they stood silently watching the pink sunlight dance on the gentle waves of the water while minarets dominated the skyline. Ananya allowed the stillness of the moment to reach the core of her being. No past, no future—only the beauty of that moment. As the sun disappeared, the moon gradually began to show her face over the horizon, like a Muslim woman shyly removing her veil. It was time for the evening prayers, and all the mosques in the area resounded with song nearly at once.

In that moment, Ananya gained a fuller understanding of how the Law of Love was operating in All That Is. All That Is was simply *allowing* its true essence of love to flow. *"All we have to do is simply be in a constant state of allowance,"* she affirmed. But she also acknowledged that while living this truth may be simple, it is not always so easy. So she would "play" with the idea and see what happens.

Ananya and her companion finally crossed back over the bridge to the European side of the city. They went to Ananya's favorite restaurant and indulged in some Turkish food as well as the most open, honest communication either one of them had ever known. They met each other often during that week in Istanbul, becoming close friends who learned to love and accept each other unconditionally. Their connection with one another was not about physical intimacy, it was about healing one another through unconditional love.

At the end of the week, it was hard to say goodbye. But Ananya was eastward bound to Bombay, India, another place she had once called home.

There is a Hindu notion that all
creation is God's play and that
the universe is one big playground.

To master human existence
is to make all of life play.

And as you explore the
grand playground that IS,

Unleash the child within you . . .

Allow your heart to sing
Allow your soul to dance

Laughter is life . . . allow
yourself to live it.

3

The Law of Completion

FOR ANYONE OF INDIAN ORIGIN, entering the Bombay airport evokes contradictory thoughts of "Ah! So good to be home!" and "What the hell am I doing here?" For Ananya, these two thoughts lived together in harmony, making her ultimately happy to be back in her native Bombay, at least for a short while.

From the airport, she went to her old family flat, which was situated on the Arabian Sea. The flat was empty now but someone had been looking after it, keeping it clean and functional. She opened the sliding glass windows and observed the familiar movie of life taking place at the shore below. It felt strange to be back, like entering into a time warp. Nothing here had changed and yet *she* had changed so completely since she'd left India years ago.

* * *

At 4:00 in the morning, Ananya awoke sensing that now-familiar presence in the room. She listened to a soft and gentle voice say, *"The 3rd Law of the Universe is the Law of Duality and Frequency. Everything in the universe has its own frequency, and these frequencies exist in duality. Light and shadow, masculine and feminine, joy and sorrow—one cannot exist without the other because they are not opposites, you see; they are two aspects of the same energy, so together they make one whole. Do you understand?"*

"Yes . . . I think I do."

"All energy in the universe consists of a manifested state and an un-manifested state. In other words, one frequency is more apparent, but both frequencies are present in all things. Every individual embodies both light and shadow. The light is the manifested state and the shadow is the hidden or un-manifested state, so the shadow does not refer to a 'dark side' of an individual. That has been a misunderstanding for many in your world. The shadow is simply the counterpoint for being whole."

"Will you say more about the shadow?"

"You will uncover more about this shadow concept throughout your journeying, just as you are remembering the Divine Laws of Healing. Now, it is for you to remember the 3rd Law of Healing, which bridges the gap to understanding the Universal Law of Duality. Remember, we walk beside you."

With that, Ananya was left to ponder the Law of Duality and Frequency. She was certainly grateful for the utter confidence that these great beings had in her. Instead of being overwhelmed by it all, she decided to just have fun, as if she was enjoying a big game or treasure hunt. Meanwhile, she was becoming even more aware that the real treasure of life lay within her own heart; she didn't need to travel anywhere in order to find it. And yet, she enjoyed the traveling; it was fun.

"Perhaps it's this energy of having fun that helps me remember the Divine Laws of Healing," she thought. *"After all, laughing and having fun opens the heart center."*

She got up to make some chai, something she simply had to have no matter where in the world she was. Ananya always made sure she brought the right spices with her on her travels . . . fresh cardamom, cinnamon, clove, star anise, nutmeg, and the secret ingredient, just a hint of saffron. As she threw the spices and the tea into the boiling water, she had to laugh at herself—she resembled a witch making her special brew.

Sitting by the window, her hot cup warming her hands, she watched the people bathing in the dirty water of the bay by the dim light of sunrise. *"There is so much poverty here,"* she thought. *"There is so much wealth, too, but it's hidden behind decorated wooden doors. The dire poverty, though, exists openly on the streets. This creates an appearance that all of India lives in poverty, which is not actually the truth of what is."* She reflected on how reality is just how we perceive it to be. *"We don't usually see things as they really are,"* she thought. *"We see things as we are."*

As she recalled the Law of Creation which states that everything is within us, Ananya was getting a deeper understanding of what that really meant. *"Nothing exists outside of our selves, not even things that we consider to be external,"* she concluded.

The sound of a ringing telephone startled her. Was something outside of her actually ringing or was this a new noise her body was making? That last thought gave her a jolt. She answered the telephone—it was a reminder that she had a breakfast date with some of her relatives.

* * *

In another part of the city as she indulged in dosas (Indian rice pancakes), Ananya sat through—rather painfully —all the family gossip. "So-and-so lost his job and wasn't that just the worst thing," and "Such-and-such a thing happened that caused a cousin's arranged marriage to be called off and wasn't that a tragedy" . . . blah, blah, blah. As far as Ananya was concerned, losing that job was the excuse (read: opportunity) so-and-so needed to finally pursue his life's dream of making music. And such-and-such a thing that happened to call off the arranged marriage was a blessing too, because she knew about the bride's secret unrequited love affair with a boy from a different caste. Now, surely, the bride was relieved about this outcome. *"Goodness gracious, the dramas!"* Ananya sighed. Well, the food tasted good anyway.

As Ananya walked back to the train station, she took a detour through a small garden to smell the flowers. Many of the bigger, more colorful flowers didn't carry much scent, but one small, insignificant-looking white flower smelled absolutely heavenly. She laughed and thought that if her relatives were here, they'd probably say, "Oh, what a pity, no color and so small . . . this flower can't be any good." They'd walk right by it, missing its intoxicating aroma. *"So many people only see the appearance of what is, and in so doing miss the significance of what truly is,"* she thought.

Suddenly she felt a wave of warm energy rush up her body and she wanted to voice what was coming from inside. Because she couldn't write it down at the moment, she decided to just talk to herself. It would look strange perhaps to people walking by, but this 3rd Law seemed to be about that anyway.

"This world we live in contains a thread of appearance and a thread of significance. The thread of appearance covers the thread of significance, so it is not always easy to see. The way to understand an event, situation, person, or flower for what it truly is—for its wholeness—is to make a commitment to go beyond the appearances of what seems to be. Appearances are but mere starting points to understanding. To stop there is to leave the understanding incomplete."

Ananya suddenly heard what came out of her mouth. She smiled because she had just remembered the 3rd Law of Healing, the Law of Completion. *"The energy of completion leads to understanding the Law of Duality. In order to truly appreciate the dual aspects inherent in All That Is, it's necessary to apply the Law of Completion."*

Ananya noted that the Law of Completion had been presenting itself all morning. "*We make all sorts of judgments and assumptions based on what we see. We call a beggar a victim, for example, but we are only seeing one tiny little scene in that person's movie. If you see only one scene of a movie, have you fully understood what the entire movie is about?*

One lifetime is like one little scene in a soul's entire movie. And every soul incarnates with intentions about how they wish to play out this particular scene. So how can we even begin to comprehend what another soul has deemed appropriate for its own evolution in a particular lifetime?

Even a murderer is also love at the core of his or her being, and has chosen to explore that essence of love by experiencing its absence first. So is it true for the one whom he or she murders. The experience is arranged and agreed upon between the two souls before incarnating; it matters not that their personalities are unaware of their agreement. If the personalities were aware, they would try to inhibit the experience, creating great conflict within the individuals concerned. The personality cannot override what the soul has already ordained.

When an innocent child suffers abuse, we consider it a great injustice, and yet we don't actually know anything about what that soul is trying to accomplish through such a life experience. So, who are we to make any sort of judgment about that situation? When we do judge, it means that our own feelings of victimization are being brought to the surface in an effort to be healed." Just then Ananya

made sense of her own childhood experience of abuse and was able to release blame.

"The truth is: There are no victims. How can there be any victims if every soul is creating the experiences it wishes to have on Earth? To call somebody a victim is to dishonor that soul and invalidate its creative power."

* * *

Ananya was grasping more about how self-empowering these Laws truly are. Once she had made her way back home, she opened the sliding glass windows, and took in a deep breath of India. As she stood in the penetrating heat of the sun, a voice came again into her head—this time as if the sun itself were speaking directly to her.

"As you are recalling the 12 Laws of Healing, you will also recall that each of the 12 is, simply, a particular frequency of love. And as you move from one to the other in your living experience, you move from one dimension of love, or one dimension of BEing to another."

"So there is a progression to these Laws?"

"There certainly is. Each Law of Healing not only addresses and therefore opens up a greater understanding of the corresponding Universal Law; each Law of Healing also provides a foundation for a deeper, more fulfilling experience of the subsequent Law of Healing. Creation opens up the experience of greater love, and love is what leads us to completion, and so on, to Law #12. However, it is important to realize that despite a progression, these Laws are always operating simultaneously."

"So they are all operating together at the same time, even though one law is building on another?"

"That is so. Have we confused you now?"

"Well . . . I'm experiencing the burden of linear thinking, I suppose."

"Imagine a rainbow. At the bottom or the foundation, you have red, followed by orange, yellow, green, blue, indigo, and then violet at the top. These colors of the rainbow show up in a distinct order, do they not?"

"They do. I've never seen one any other way."

"So, there is an order. And yet all the colors are there, simultaneously, which is what makes it a rainbow. If the colors were showing separately in the sky, it would no longer be a rainbow."

Ananya got it now. It's about seeing the whole energy and not just a part of it. "Now, what follows the Law of Completion?" she wondered.

4

The Law of Manifestation

THE TRAINS IN INDIA are something to experience. Ananya relished this 2nd class sleeper car experience as her every sense was activated by the colors, the sounds, the smells! Oh, the smells! She loved the mountains and never missed a chance to go trekking. For this reason, she and her friend, Akash, were on their way up to the Himalayan foothills. They both shared a deep appreciation for the mountains' compelling beauty as well as their sacred silence.

The ranting and raving of the tea and snack sellers finally dissipated like a loud choir tired of its song. It was nearly midnight and people starting settling into their berths for the night. Three berths were stacked one on top of the other, and Akash and Ananya lay on top adjacent berths, which are considered good because the higher the berth, the safer one was from getting visited by nocturnal thieves.

But Ananya didn't fear thieves; she feared snorers. She quickly assessed the people around her, wondering which ones might keep her awake all night with their snoring. Ananya had made similar train journeys many times and had yet to experience one during which she'd actually slept. Someone always snored—and earplugs didn't help.

Several hours had passed, and sure enough, a roar emanated from the lowest bunk on the opposite side. *"Why did this always happen, without fail?"* she thought. Ananya looked over at Akash who was sleeping soundly. Resigned to her sleepless fate, she decided to meditate.

Before long, she felt the humming vibration again around her heart center.

"The 4th Universal Law is the Law of Attraction. You already know that everything has its own frequency. And like frequencies attract one another. Essentially, one attracts the same frequency of who one BE."

"So, everything in one's life is merely a reflection of one's own energy?"

"That is so. If one is being fearful, what do you think that individual is going to attract?"

"Whatever it is he or she fears."

"Exactly—fear is an extremely powerful magnet, as is love. The 4th Law of Healing can be applied to address this matter of attraction. There is someone whom you will meet in the mountains who will assist you to recall this Law. As always, we walk beside you."

* * *

Ananya felt a hand on her arm. "Anu, wake up, we're here." She felt like she'd been sleeping for only five minutes, but was glad they had arrived. After a bite to eat, the two friends took a jeep into the mountains—another days' journey—until they reached the last village which was accessible by road. There, they would spend the night in a government rest house and begin trekking at dawn.

As they rolled out their sleeping bags on the cots provided, Ananya thought about the Law of Attraction. *"I was told I would meet someone here in the mountains that would trigger my memory of the next Law of Healing,"* she told Akash, who, by now, had been fully informed on her adventure.

"Really? How? Where?" Akash was fascinated.

"I don't know, Akash, but I've been learning about divine perfection and to trust in All That Is. I have faith that we won't have to do anything at all. We shall simply BE, and this person shall find us." Ananya had confidence that everything would fall into place.

The night air grew colder and both felt quite tired from their traveling. To keep their heads warm, they donned monkey caps, made fun of each other for how silly they looked, and then crawled into their sleeping bags for the night.

* * *

They stepped on to the trail at the crack of dawn. It was a gorgeous day, with a fresh coat of snow adorning the peaks.

"My lungs don't know what to do with this air, it's so clean," Akash proclaimed as he took a deep breath. Ananya, though, was slightly distracted by her human instincts kicking in. *"Yeah . . . I don't mean to be a fuss-pot or anything, but I could really go for a cup of chai right now."*

Akash chuckled and assured her they would probably find a villager who could make them some up ahead.

Turning a corner, Akash noticed cows grazing in the clearing. "See? That means there are people here . . . hey, do you hear that?"

They heard the sound of people crying. As they neared the source of the sound, they saw a man and a woman sitting on the ground crying while a child lay on a cot inside a modest hut. They approached the hut and offered help. The man explained that their only son was sick with very high fever and they couldn't afford to pay for his treatment. They were afraid they might lose him.

Ananya walked over and looked into the little boy's eyes. It took every ounce of energy he had to return her gaze, but there was instant recognition. Ananya knew this was the one who would help her to remember the 4th Law of Healing.

Some higher instinct took over and she placed her hands a few inches above various points on the boy's head, feet, and solar plexus. Her body seemed to move and act on its own, according to what the boy's own energy field needed. She gave the boy energetic treatment like a surgeon performing her one-millionth operation, even though she wasn't touching the boy at all. She just *knew* what to do. Although her mind couldn't logically grasp what was occurring, her inner knowing told her that she was simply acting as a conduit for the boy to transmute his own frequency back to wellness.

The boy began to moan and cry from pain. His mother ran over to him and asked Ananya what was happening. To answer, Ananya allowed her inner voice to speak out loud.

"It seems your son has a virus . . . I . . . I can actually see it. Everything is energy—such as this virus—and it is possible to see energy . . . to feel it, to hear it in some cases . . . even smell it. So, umm . . . .emotion, for example, is simply energy in motion—e-motion—and if you move enough energy, you eventually create matter. That's why a negative emotion left unresolved often materializes as physical disease."

The mother's eyes got wide. Ananya continued to explain to the parents as best she could what she was observing in their son.

"I'm sensing that your son got very angry about something, but instead of expressing it, he held it inside. This threw him off balance, altering his healthy frequency to a dis-eased one"

The parents were astonished "How did you know that?" They admitted they had been fighting a lot with one another in front of their son, even though they felt it must be upsetting for him.

"I don't know," she admitted *"I just felt it when I tuned into his energy field. A virus gets attracted to a particular vibratory environment. At this time, that environment is*

your son's body. So the immediate solution in this case, is to transmute the vibratory environment so that it is no longer attractive for the virus. I am not giving or even taking anything away. I am, through energetic facilitation, helping your son transmute his current frequency so that it no longer matches the frequency of the virus. That way, the vibratory environment becomes hostile for the virus to live in. As a consequence, the virus will naturally leave his body. However, during that release, his pain will intensify before it subsides. Now, as for your son's anger, that will still need to be addressed once his physical body regains some strength. If it is not addressed, this or even some other illness could reoccur."

Both mother and father sat quietly by their son's side, praying. Ananya was astonished at the trust they seemed to have in her, a perfect stranger just passing by. *She* knew that this was no coincidence, that in fact there were no coincidences in life. Did these villagers know that, too?

Ananya watched the boy's body as she continued to work with him. She could see three distinct energy pathways running from his head to his toes and back up to the head again. Each one flowed in a different way and each one had its own color.

The first appeared yellow and ran up and down his body in what looked like three lines, beginning above his head and reaching a bit beyond his feet. The second appeared green and ran in a circular, spiral motion also up and down the boy's body in both directions. The third appeared royal blue and began from below his feet. Two lines of blue zigzagged and crisscrossed one another, rising up his body until they met somewhere above his head.

Ananya noticed these lines appeared faint in certain areas, but as she continued to pass energy over the boy, she saw these same lines get brighter. The color slowly became more vivid.

An inspiration came from the depths of her belly: *"These pathways are the manifestation of one's consciousness! They are also somehow showing a mirror reflection of the consciousness of All That Is. We are a part of All That Is, and All That Is, is a part of us,"* she thought. Ananya recognized these three pathways as a key to healing, because true healing doesn't take place in the body, but in the *consciousness* of the individual.

She glanced over at the boy's father to notice if she could see these same lines or pathways in him. She did. Same with the boy's mother, same with Akash. All three pathways were present in each person—all with the same colors—but with the quality and consistency of the lines varying from one individual to another.

Finally, after twitching and moaning for half an hour, the boy broke out in a sweat. His fever had finally broken and he went quietly to sleep.

Slowly, Ananya stood up. The boy's father thanked her profusely. "Oh, he is going to be alright! How can I repay you? I don't have money but I must give you something!" the man insisted.

Ananya smiled and said, *"Well, if you would be so kind as to make us some chai, I would be most grateful!"* His

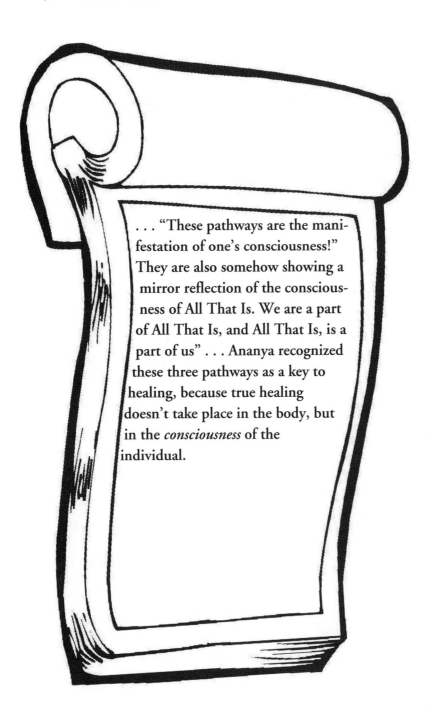

. . . "These pathways are the manifestation of one's consciousness!"
They are also somehow showing a
mirror reflection of the consciousness of All That Is. We are a part
of All That Is, and All That Is, is a
part of us" . . . Ananya recognized
these three pathways as a key to
healing, because true healing
doesn't take place in the body, but
in the *consciousness* of the
individual.

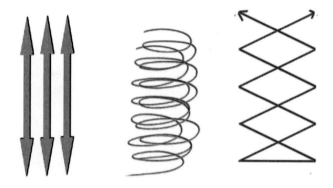

THE 3 PATHWAYS
OF CONSCIOUSNESS

wife leaped up and went scurrying into their tiny kitchen while Ananya took time for herself several meters away. She just needed to review things in her mind.

What had just taken place was alchemy. Alchemy is based on the principle of transmutation, which is "recreate the energy, recreate the manifestation of matter." By recreating the energy, one automatically recreates whatever one is attracting. Ananya recalled that the Law of Manifestation is the 4th Law of Healing that addresses the Law of Attraction.

The Law of Manifestation governs how things are materialized into physical form. "As above, so below." That means that whatever exists physically also exists energetically and vice versa. In fact, the whole universe is manifested in each and every human being. So, we are each a tiny universe within ourselves, a mini hologram of All That Is.

Ananya had always held the opinion that conventional western medicine was nothing more than big business. It wasn't about health; it was about money. Only now was she gaining the insight as to why she had always felt so strongly about this issue. Conventional medicine was based on suppressing symptoms, which throws off the natural equilibrium of the body. *"It's like watering the leaves of the plant instead of the roots,"* she thought. *"Wet leaves might give the appearance of being healthier, but in reality, if the roots remain dry and thirsty, eventually the plant will still wither and die."* Most of today's doctors only seem to understand the leaf, not the root, and that is why so many illnesses reoccur. Ananya always understood this concept, but now, finally, the pieces of the puzzle were coming together as to *why* she always understood this.

The boy's mother came outside with a pot of chai and some hot food. After refueling, the two trekkers excused themselves, knowing they still had many hours walk to go before reaching the next rest house where they'd be able to stay the night. Before they left, Ananya walked over to the boy who was resting peacefully. She silently blessed him.

* * *

They continued on through a dense forest as the sound of thunder echoed through the valley. *"Oh, I adore thunderstorms!"* Ananya announced excitedly. As it began to rain, the two took shelter under a big over-hanging piece of rock.

Akash's curiosity got the better of him. "Anu, how on earth did you know how to heal that boy? I mean, you're a writer . . . did you study these things somewhere? Have you taken a course of some kind?"

"Akash, such a thing is not to be learned. It's only to be remembered. The presence of that little boy and his situation triggered something that was already inside of me. You know, I think everyone on this earth is a healer of one kind or another."

"You do?"

"Absolutely. Healing is everything, and it can be expressed in many different ways."

"How do you mean?"

"Think about it. When I'm feeling low, you take my hand and give me a warm reassuring smile, don't you?"

Akash nodded.

"So, that smile of yours has the ability to make a difference in my life at that moment. You are a healer with your smile."

"Okay, I get your point, but what *you* did . . . "

"I may have made a difference for that boy, just like your smile makes a difference for me, but he healed himself. All healing is self-healing, though sometimes some assistance is required. You know, I think doubt is just as powerful as faith. Even the faintest of doubts can sabotage one's healing process. The great thing about children is that they have no doubts, no preconceived beliefs to limit them. They have faith because they know they are innocent."

* * *

Akash and Ananya experienced the ups and downs of the next several days . . . the beauty, the serenity, the fatigue, the cold; the desire to wash their bodies, but their inability to do so. On the way back, just before reaching the village where they had spent their first night, the path they had taken now had a different face on it. A recent landslide left behind a treacherous mountain of dirt and unstable rocks that they had to climb over.

Akash was tired and irritable. "Why this, why now?" he grumbled. Ananya was equally exhausted but found that she was able to now attune to the energy of the Laws, even the ones she had not yet remembered consciously.

"Akash, don't ask 'why' . . . ask 'what.'"

"Huh?"

"Perhaps the question to ask is not, 'Why is this happening?' but instead, 'What is right about this situation?'"

"Okay, Anu, I'm certainly curious about what could possibly be right about this!" They sat down to rest before deciding on their next step.

Ananya must have dozed off because when she opened her eyes, she saw a donkey's leg in front of her face. She looked up. The same little boy she had helped days before sat atop a donkey and waved at her to get on. The boy skillfully maneuvered the donkey across the landslide, first taking Ananya and then returning to take Akash. She was so thrilled to see this boy again, looking healthy and happy. *"It's true that what goes around comes around,"* she thought. And the help that she had given him came back unexpectedly at just the right moment.

The Law of Manifestation is the dimension of being where perceptions are transmuted into trust and fear is transmuted into love.

Another long train ride brought them back to Bombay. After a couple of days of rest, Ananya would be heading to the Kingdom of Thailand.

5

The Law of Evolution

"**S**AWADEE KAA!" THE OWNER of the guesthouse chirped as Ananya arrived at her destination, north of Chiang Mai in the Mae Hong Song province. She so loved the serenity of Thailand. And she chose to stay in a very simple yet comfortable wooden hut by the river. This peaceful place was conducive to quiet reflection, which is exactly what Ananya needed at this moment.

She found herself in a small, interesting town full of contrasting flavors and colors. It included a Buddhist community, a Muslim community, as well as a community of foreigners—mostly Christian westerners—living together harmoniously. "*A place like this with such contrast of peoples, beliefs, and customs coexisting peacefully is destined for greatness,*" she thought.

She rented a motorbike and went for a ride around the area. With the rainy season under way in Thailand, the clouds hung low over the emerald green hills. She decided to ride to natural hot springs just outside of town where 80-degree (centigrade) water was bubbling up from the earth. Ananya sat down beside the spring, closed her eyes, and with every exhalation of her breath, focused on sending loving energy toward the core of Mother Earth.

Her heart center began to vibrate again with a warm, humming sensation. A few seconds later she heard a deep, tender voice in her head.

"The 5th Law of the Universe is the Law of Contrast. Contrasts of energy facilitate growth."

"What is the difference between contrast and duality?"

"Duality is about the two aspects or the two frequencies that constitute one whole energy. Contrast, on the other hand, is about two or more distinct energies. There is a small creature, easy to spot in this part of Thailand, which can teach you more about this Law, as well as the corresponding Law of Healing that applies. Remember, we walk beside you."

Ananya had learned that she needn't seek for anything. Instead, her soul attracted exactly what it needed at the appropriate moment in time. Relaxed with that thought, she decided to take a soak downstream where the water temperature was more moderate.

* * *

Riding back from the hot springs, cheeks beet red from her soak, Ananya passed through huge fields that had been burnt absolutely black. She felt compelled to stop in front of one of them.

She thought about how farmers understand how to cause new growth, which is why they periodically destroy their fields by burning them. The destruction is necessary to allow new, fertile soil just underneath the surface to produce new crops. She noticed the contrast between the burnt field and a newly sprouting one in the distance. To her, they represented the cycle of death and birth necessary for the growth and evolution of All That Is. By this time her body was buzzing with waves of energy again as she remembered that the 5th Law of Healing is the Law of Evolution.

As she gazed at the ground, she noticed three beetles, which symbolize transformation in Egypt. Three beetles represent the evolutionary cycle: birth, life, and death. Ananya reveled in how magically everything at every moment demonstrates the Divine Laws. She now knew that everything around her and in her *is* the living Laws. The great beings had spoken of this, she recalled, but now a deeper understanding bubbled up within her—an awareness at the heart level. *"We are the living Laws, All That Is is the living Laws, manifesting itself at every moment, everywhere."*

It dawned on her that through her own process of personal evolution, she already *is* what she had been trying to become. Like the new soil that lay underneath the old soil, it was just waiting for the right moment to give birth to new growth. It didn't suddenly appear out of nowhere; *it was there all the time! "We are already what we are trying to become. So that's why there is never anything to do . . . there is only to BE."* Then she recognized how this and every Law relates back to the one big Law, the Law of Being and Creation. *"It's impossible to separate the Laws from one another; they're so tightly interconnected, just like the heart of All That Is,"* she concluded.

But she wondered why it always seemed to take catastrophic events in life for transformation to occur. Then, as if coming from the beetles, she heard *"A state of perfection is not a state of growth. Change doesn't occur when things are happy and peaceful. A disturbance of the energy needs to happen to allow a release to occur—the destruction which gives birth to new life."* She realized that such a release is like the burning of the fields—a necessary part of the life cycle and a prerequisite to completing transformation and evolution.

Just then, a butterfly flew in front of Ananya's face as if to offer confirmation of this magical process. *"Ah, this is the small creature they were talking about"* she recalled, because she already was aware that when a caterpillar becomes complete in its cocoon, it actually disintegrates itself into goo. From that goo, a beautiful butterfly emerges. *"What a perfect example of how evolution leads to contrast,"* she thought. Ananya, too, could feel herself disintegrating and reintegrating at the same time. It seemed a never-ending process.

6

The Law of Free Will

EVERY MORNING, ANANYA AWOKE to the sound of rain pelting the wooden roof of her bungalow. She found the sound intoxicating and allowed herself to lie in bed so it could permeate her. She balanced her days in Thailand between writing and quiet meditation, interspersed with eating spicy hot curries and socializing with the local townspeople.

One night, the clouds had lifted after heavy rains and the air was pleasantly cool. Ananya sat out on the little wooden veranda, lit a candle and watched the stars. They seemed boundless and infinite—always there, even when one could not actually see them. The abundance of stars in the sky reminded her of the absolute limitlessness of the universe. *"Just like the great beings that are always 'walking beside' me,"* she thought.

A gentle breeze blew in and the air temperature instantly got warmer. She felt the familiar vibration around her heart center.

"We see you have understood the 6th Law of the Universe."

"I have?"

"Yes, it is the Law of Abundance. The universe is infinitely abundant—in everything. There is no lack of any kind in the universe. Do you see?"

"Yes, the stars were showing me that . . . but, I don't understand one thing. If the universe is so abundant, then what about the countless people who experience lack in so many different ways: financial, physical, and so on?"

"They are experiencing an abundance of lack. Abundance does not only mean an abundance of wealth or abundance of health; abundance simply means abundance. One could experience an abundance of poverty or an abundance of sickness. And those are not random situations. God does not say, 'I think I'll make this one sick and this one healthy.' That is not how it works. Abundance means ample supply, and anything and everything is abundantly available in the universe.

If one wishes to understand more about the current abundance in one's life, the 6th Law of Healing may be applied. This 6th Law is another one of the primary laws in operation. As always, we walk beside you."

Ananya had never thought of abundance in that way before. She guessed that this Law of Healing, which explains how abundance operates, has to do with the fact that one's abundance isn't random.

The breeze rustled the leaves on the tree outside her balcony and made the candle flame dance. Even though beauty surrounded her, Ananya felt alone—an aloneness that was, perhaps, the only "lack" she was experiencing at this point in her life. She lived the kind of life many envied and admired because of her ability to go wherever she wanted, whenever she wanted. Ananya truly enjoyed her life, but she wanted a partner to share it with.

She often wondered if God really wanted her to be alone. Could that be the divine plan for her life? But then it didn't feel right to concede to God saying "Well, thy will be done" if she didn't accept what she perceived as "God's plan" for her.

As she continued to watch the stars, a small snake appeared on the ledge of the veranda. It appeared to be a harmless one. *"So, Mr. Snake, what do you think? Do you think God's plan is for me to be alone all my life?"*

She thought she was hallucinating when the snake actually turned itself toward her and replied telepathically.

"Why would God want you to be alone, my child? You have willed your current situation. The power to change it lies within you and only you. Even God cannot interfere with your will."

"Even God cannot interfere with my will? Now that's a powerful concept, especially coming from a talking snake."

Suddenly, her remembrance of the 6th Law of Healing took priority over this interaction. Ananya excused herself from her slithery friend to go inside and write down her reflections.

The Law of Free Will is the 6th Divine Law of Healing, addressing the Universal Law of Abundance. How one experiences abundance in life relates to how one exercises free will—for this planet uniquely operates on a Law of Free Will.

Ananya clearly saw how this Law was operating in her life, though it was tough to swallow. After falling into the same self-denying pattern one too many times in her relationships, she *subconsciously* decided that the surest way to prevent that pattern from repeating was to avoid relationships all together. Therefore she'd willed the aloneness she was experiencing. Wanting to have a partner to fill emptiness within, only affirms one's lack. And as she already learned from Law #4, like attracts like, therefore, lack can only attract more lack.

One's abundance lies wherever one's energy is focused. Ananya had put her energy toward avoiding a pattern she didn't want to fall into again. Yet, while she successfully evaded the issue at hand, it was still her responsibility to address the issue *within* her that attracted the same reoccurring pattern in her life. Once she could acknowledge the belief or the judgment that exists underneath the pattern, then she could choose to release it—and then exercise her free will to make new choices.

Ananya acknowledged that it is not God who is willing her fate. Rather, it is—and had always been—*her* willing her own fate. Free will means that we are completely and totally responsible for our own lives. There is nothing and no one to either blame or thank for our current abundance, whatever that may be. It also means that we are empowered to make different choices, according to our will, every single step of the way.

She listened to the sound of the frogs and geckos outside. Suddenly she didn't feel alone anymore, and she felt like praying to God *"Thy will be done."*

Ananya went back out to the veranda to find the wise snake that had assisted her to recall this Law, but he was gone. She was once again awed by how All That Is seemed to be responding instantly to her thoughts, her words . . . her needs. She realized that many such as her would get stuck in this matter of "My will" versus "Thy will"; "Thy will" is perceived as being something outside of ourselves, when in fact "My will" and "Thy will" are exactly the same thing. **Ananya now could recognize that trusting in the divine plan of the universe is synonymous with trusting in one's self, because we are the creators who will the divine plan of our lives and of the universe.**

* * *

Ananya's journey was at the half-way point now and, though she felt quite comfortable in Thailand, her inner knowing told her to explore and experience other places. And besides, there were still six more laws to remember. So she packed her things and slowly made way for Bangkok, where she would catch her next flight headed for Tokyo, Japan.

The time spent in Thailand had been extremely healing for Ananya and she left feeling more unified than when she had come. As her outward journey coincided with her inward journey, the Laws of Healing seemed to be progressing from outer to inner as well.

7

The Law of Equality

AFTER EXPERIENCING THE TRANQUILITY of northern Thailand, the hustle and bustle of Tokyo - where she had attended University many years ago—came as a bit of a shock to Ananya. Yet, the familiarity was there. She planned to stay there only a few days with her old college mate, Yoko.

In the evening, the two women walked the streets of Shibuya, in the heart of the city. Hundreds of expressionless suits and ties swarmed around them with definite destinations in mind. Ananya had always been fascinated by the cultural conditioning in Japan that clearly defined social norms of behavior—sometimes at the expense of individual expression.

Nearby, a loud commotion erupted at a corner of a busy intersection. A middle-aged man, probably a bit drunk, stripped down to his birthday suit while shouting unintelligible things to passers-by who tried their best to ignore the man's existence. It didn't take long for police to grab the man and take him away. Although his behavior was inappropriate, both Yoko and Ananya felt uncomfortable about the way he was being treated, like he was inferior. This was only one man. Indeed, entire communities throughout history were deemed inferior by those with distorted visions of their own superiority.

Ready to head home, the two squeezed into an overly crowded subway car. With warm bodies pressing up against her on every side, Ananya again felt the gentle humming sensation around her heart center. *"What timing!"* she thought sarcastically. *"Are we really going to this now?"*

The voice that came in her head this time was sweet and more feminine than some of the others. *"Is it an inappropriate time?"*

Ananya was amazed there was no limit to the presence of these great beings and their communication with her. They certainly had no concept of time or space. She couldn't hide her smile, so she silently agreed to give it a try. *"I guess there's a point here somewhere,"* she thought.

The voice continued, *"The 7th Law of the Universe is the Law of Limitations. Now, if the Laws are all about breaking through personal limitations, how is there a Law of Limitation, you may wonder."*

"I am wondering, yes."

"Well, the limitation this Law refers to is appropriateness."

"Appropriateness?"

"Please close your eyes for a moment."

She did and, like a dream, she saw wild animals running across the African plains. Some animals were very powerful, others were more delicate, and yet clearly they were all equally important for the ecosystem of the plain. She saw that the lion will always conquer the gazelle; it is the way of the wild and entirely appropriate. However, these two creatures know that they are equal in that scenario. The lion is not better than the gazelle; the lion is simply playing out its role, and so is the gazelle.

Ananya opened her eyes. They had reached their stop, so they piled out, walked to Yoko's place, and settled in for the night. After a bit of chit-chat, they both fell asleep on their futons. But Ananya awoke after only a short time. The clock read 2:22 a.m. Unable to sleep, she got out her laptop, reviewed her writings about the six previous Laws, and then reflected on the images of the wild animals she was shown earlier.

She realized that the animal kingdom lived in total harmony with the Laws of the Universe. *"If animals can understand their equal roles in All That Is, surely we should be able to,"* she pondered. Waves of energy were running through her body again. *"Equality,"* she whispered to herself. The Law of Equality is the 7th Law of Healing which addresses the Universal Law of Limitations. All That Is is equal. No one is superior to another. And while we each play out our appropriate roles in life, we must always remember that we are all absolutely equal.

* * *

During the next few days, Ananya wandered around the familiar Japanese city with an empty mind. She had now recalled seven of the Divine Laws of Healing and wanted to take a break from contemplating them. She wanted to just BE.

Without any plan or agenda, she allowed her impulses to guide her. One such impulse led her into a tucked-away sushi bar. At this odd time of the day, only one other person was sitting at the bar. She sat down and picked out some of her favorites like sea water eel, a delicacy she had grown to like during her student days.

The other person, a young Japanese man on the next seat at the bar, watched Ananya for a while from the corner of his eye. He debated whether to grab this opportunity to practice his English with a foreigner.

Several cups of sake later, he finally leaned over and said, "Hello." Because Ananya could see energy, she had seen this man's energy being drawn to hers. She knew there must be a reason for it, and was happy to engage him in conversation. His interest was thoroughly peaked once he learned that she had been writing about the Divine Laws of Healing.

Before long, he found himself sharing his deepest secret with Ananya. A gay man, he had contracted the HIV virus from his last partner nearly ten years ago. Since then, he had felt so guilty and ashamed of himself that he lived like a recluse. He spoke of how he used to be a respected man in the community. For that reason, he had always kept his sexual orientation a secret from everyone; even though it ate him up inside. He judged himself a "bad" person and now he was sick.

Ananya intuitively felt that this man's deadly illness was nothing more than a physical manifestation of his feelings of guilt and shame. She shared this thought with him. Perhaps his perception that he wasn't equal to others was holding him in this prison of dis-ease, she suggested. In his mind, his judgment about himself as a bad person placed him in an inferior position to others—others are "good" while he is "bad." She explained that when one is willing to break through the limitations of perception and belief, absolutely *anything* is possible—even the total disappearance of a life-threatening illness.

The young man was willing to consider that this could be true.

At his request, Ananya continued to speak whatever came from deep within her. *"Since all is equal, there can be no 'good' or 'bad.' Good or bad implies judgment. And where there's judgment, there's idleness of energy, which causes dis-ease. For example, if a smoker wants to quit but at some level of his being he judges himself for smoking, it's unlikely he'll be able to quit. What one resists, persists."*

The young man sat silently for a few moments, integrating the profound discussion he was having with this foreign woman in a lonely sushi bar. He was in a process of deep healing—at the *mental* level. Ananya understood this by the way he looked at her now. It was the first and most important step for his recovery.

She asked for her check and added, "*If one has to quan-tify things, then perhaps it's possible to say there is 'good' and 'another form of good.' That 'other form of good' may be dressed in different clothing and give an appearance of 'bad', but it is still a part of All That Is.*"

The young man was apologetic for taking up so much of Ananya's time and graciously thanked her for sharing her wisdom. He called her a guru! That word made her cringe and she quickly corrected the young man. "*Please, I don't believe in gurus. Some people come along and offer assistance, guidance, and encouragement. However, you are your own master. You teach the student within you every moment. And that student, in turn, teaches that master within you every moment.*"

* * *

Back in Yoko's apartment, Ananya sat down with her laptop again. So much wisdom seemed to be emerging from somewhere deep inside of her that she felt the need to write it all out.

Unless one understands the judgments one holds about oneself, one cannot feel emotionally complete. It's judgment that inhibits the sense of being at one with All That Is. That means the moment a person makes a judgment, it separates him or her from every other individual and All That Is. Judg-ment is a betrayal of the soul. It destroys equality.

Many people implement guilt in their lives as a preven-tative method, a way to avoid repeating wrongful acts; 'wrongful' being a perception of course. The young Japanese man held the perception that he had done something "wrong" and was therefore "bad." This perception led him to ensure, in the most self-destructive way possible, that he could never ever do it again. If All That Is is equal, then there really is no 'wrong' way of going about things, just as there is no 'right' way. There is only a way.

As an example, the subway station was several blocks away from the sushi bar. But there wasn't only one way to get from there to the station. Some people took the direct route; others diverged and went through the market street. Many get distracted and miss the train that others have already caught. But it doesn't matter. They simply catch the next train or the one after that. Similarly, people embark on different journeys to ultimately reach the same destination. Each soul walks its own path, and each path is equal. So, whichever path is chosen is entirely appropriate for that soul, at that moment.

* * *

Ananya packed her things—again—as she would be flying to New Zealand the following morning. Yoko reminded her about a necklace she left lying on the kitchen table—an Andean Cross which was given to her in Peru. As she picked it up she felt that gentle humming vibration around her heart again. As if someone was whispering in her ear ever so softly, she heard *"12 Laws, 12 Dimensions, 12 Bodies . . . all equal."*

"12 bodies???" she asked herself. She looked again at her Andean Cross, which is the Incan symbol for All That Is, and—like a flash—received an illumination about 11 "energy bodies" that, together with our physical body, make up who we are. She saw very clearly that each of us is so much more than we can possibly imagine.

Ananya quickly grabbed a pen and paper to note down what she "saw".

The *Physical body* is the vehicle in which we carry all the other bodies.

The *Biological body* carries the record of all physical experiences—such as trauma, injury and illness— throughout our numerous lifetimes. It even carries the record of physical structure and appearance from other incarnations.

The *Etheric body* is what many refer to as the "aura" of a person. It's a colorful energy body visible to the at- tuned naked eye.

The *Infra-red body* is much harder to see and contains all of our DNA coding.

The *Emotional body* carries all the emotions we have ever experienced.

The *Mental body* carries all the beliefs we hold about ourselves and the world around us.

The *Causal body* is the body that carries our karma from this and all lifetimes.

The *Astral body* is where our consciousness begins to exist multi-dimensionally, beyond time and space. It is the dream state.

The *Soul body* is what some refer to as "the higher self." It is the soul.

The *Sound body* is the part of our consciousness that resonates as a sound vibration throughout All That Is. This is why certain sounds can have such a healing effect; they work at a high level of our being.

The *Light body* is the part of our consciousness that is pure light.

The *Collective body* is the part of our consciousness that is at one with the collective consciousness of All That Is.

All of these aspects made up the rainbow that is us. And since all the bodies, just like all 12 Laws, were equal and inseparable from one another, then whatever is found in the collective body can be found, to some degree, in the physical body as well, and vice versa. This gave further insight to Ananya about just how interconnected everything and everyone is.

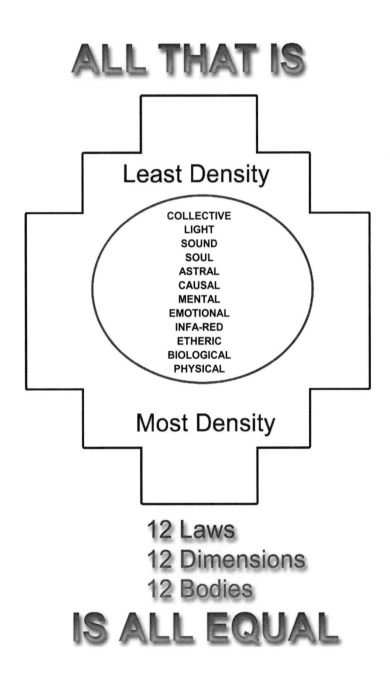

ALL THAT IS

Least Density

COLLECTIVE
LIGHT
SOUND
SOUL
ASTRAL
CAUSAL
MENTAL
EMOTIONAL
INFA-RED
ETHERIC
BIOLOGICAL
PHYSICAL

Most Density

12 Laws
12 Dimensions
12 Bodies

IS ALL EQUAL

After Ananya said good-bye to her friend Yoko, she began looking forward to going back to New Zealand, where she had once stayed for a brief period of time. She sensed that she was about to hit a turning point in her life (as if it hadn't already taken enough turns). She was getting closer to rediscovering all of the Divine Laws of Healing, and in the process of rediscovery, she realized she had been *living* all the Laws in one form or another.

Her inward journey persisted as her outward journey continued into its eighth week; A journey that had really begun long before that.

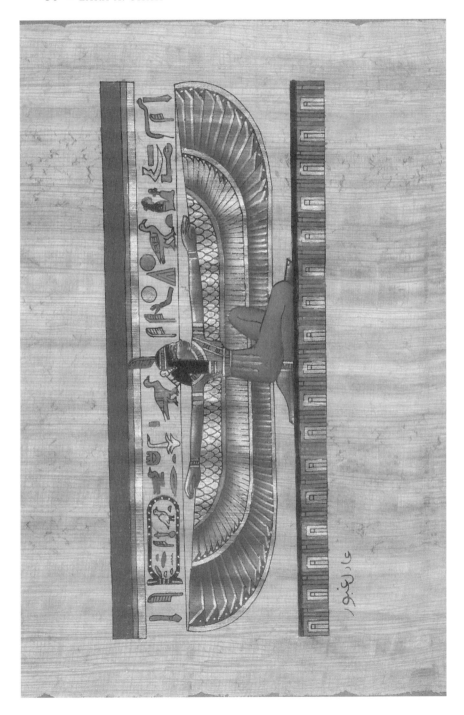

8

The Law of Ma'at (Balance)

ON THE SOUTH ISLAND OF New Zealand, Ananya checked herself into a bed & breakfast in Kaikoura, a place where rugged mountains sharply meet the Pacific Ocean and dolphins play close to the shore. Ananya considered taking extra time here in New Zealand. Besides, she had mixed feelings about going home. She had always loved her job, but now, suddenly, she wasn't sure if it fit anymore.

It became clear that she was—and had always been—a master healer, as well as a teacher. And yet, she felt great resistance to the idea of quitting her job. Throughout this journey, she had recalled vivid past-life memories of being persecuted and killed for teaching her truth. What if people judged her like that again? What if she failed? The force pushing her to step more into her true BEing was overwhelming. But did she really want to pay the possible price?

"Staying with my comfortable writing job certainly seems the easier choice," she thought. It didn't feel right, she had to admit, just felt more comfortable.

She took out the papyrus painting she had been carrying with her for the past two months. Ma'at's blue eyes almost seemed to say to her, *"To thine own self be true."* Ananya stopped and took a deep breath.

All the movement of the previous weeks had caused the scale to tip too far in one direction, leaving her feeling a bit unbalanced. Yet, after all she had learned, she understood the uselessness of worrying about anything, so she ventured out for a walk along the ocean.

After walking for an hour, she reached a quiet little cove where she noticed a pod of dolphins playing close to shore. Excited, she stood and watched them doing backward somersaults in the air. *"Oh, what fabulous creatures they are,"* she thought, with deep admiration. Here she was, concerned with what to do next with her life and in front of her were playful dolphins, so joyful and carefree. She silently thanked them for reminding her to just BE.

Here was the perfect spot for meditation, so Ananya stood at the edge of the water, closed her eyes, and took some deep breaths as she stayed connected with the dolphins.

She immediately felt the humming vibration again around her heart center, though it was subtle this time. The voice she heard was soft and playful.

"The 8th Universal Law is the Law of Choice. There is always a choice in the universe. As for us, we choose to play most of the time."

"What is the difference between choice and free will?"

"Well, first one needs to understand that one has a choice before one can exercise free will in that choice."

"Oh . . . I see . . . okay"

"As you know, each Law of Healing corresponds with a Universal Law. You are now seeing how the Universal Laws facilitate the Laws of Healing too. When there is resistance to the Universal Law of Choice, such as indecision or procrastination, the 8th Law of Healing can set one free."

Ananya had to accept that she was presently stuck at this particular Law. She knew she needed to move through this next Law of Healing herself before she could fully become conscious of it. She requested assistance from the great beings that walk beside her.

Once she had gradually opened her eyes, she saw the dolphins had swum farther offshore. Suddenly, the misty outline of a huge winged creature appeared ten feet in front of her. It resembled a condor that was as big as a building. Ananya began to cry when she recognized who she was seeing.

"I am Ma'at, Goddess of Truth and Justice," the creature said in an even, balanced tone. *"Why, my child, are you stuck? Be present in your own truth, and the choice will always make itself known to you."*

Ananya fell to her knees before Ma'at, the one whose painting she had been carrying around, the one she deeply resonated with without understanding why.

Without a change in her tone, Ma'at asked, *"Why do you fall to your knees, my child?"*

"I am overwhelmed by your awesome presence before me."

"You are just as awesome as I. And as you already have learned, you and I are equals. So if you insist on being on your knees, then I must also be on my knees."

At that moment Ananya saw the magnificent wings of Ma'at fold while she got down on one knee and bowed her head. Ananya wondered if words would ever be able to describe this experience. Probably not, she quickly concluded, as she took another deep breath.

Ma'at lifted her head and said *"Do not be afraid of your own greatness, my child. Be humbled by it."*

Ananya was utterly speechless.

Ma'at guided her through an exercise, engaging the heart center—where one's truth resides—as a scale. She asked Ananya to imagine the possible choices in front of her: One was to continue with her current job; another was to quit her job to pursue spiritual healing and teaching. She then suggested Ananya place each possibility in two imagined crystal balls. She then "placed" each crystal ball on Ananya's heart center and asked her to observe whether the sensation she felt in the heart area was one of expansion or contraction, whether it felt heavy or light. Ma'at explained that a ball that produces the sensation of lightness and expansion resonates in harmony with one's BEing. A ball that feels heavy and causes contraction does not. Once Ananya's mind was completely disengaged from the decision process and she could fully acknowledge the truth in her heart, the answer became obvious. The choice was actually made *for* her.

Ma'at whispered gently, *"When one follows one's truth and shows justice toward one's own soul, then the question of choice is easily addressed."* With a calm and peaceful smile, she continued, *"The definition of health is simply to be true to one's self."* Then she unfolded her multicolored wings and disappeared from Ananya's vision.

Still glowing from the experience, Ananya decided to quit her job and dive into the unknown. As soon as she made her decision, she felt her balance return. She became more conscious of her breath; it was now slower and deeper. It was then she realized that while her mind had been occupied with her indecision, she had been taking shallow breaths. *"It probably works both ways,"* she thought. *"Shallow breathing often keeps people from really being in touch with their own truth."*

* * *

When Ananya returned to her room, she studied the painting of Ma'at. *"The painting doesn't do her justice,"* she thought.

Then, with total ease and clarity she remembered that the Law of Ma'at is the 8th Divine Law of Healing, addressing the Universal Law of Choice.

She began to write . . .

The Law of Ma'at is about truth, justice, and balance. It could also be called the Law of Balance. Once one understands Law #7, the equality of All That Is, then it's possible to appreciate how All That Is seeks to maintain balance. When one is in truth, then one is in balance, in harmony.

The Law of Ma'at is the Law that all things are based on, because all things are constantly striving to achieve and maintain balance. What is balance for one, however, is not necessarily balance for another. For example, one kind of plant needs sunlight and water every day to maintain its balance, while another requires sunlight and water only once a week to maintain its balance.

For us, balance is an individual thing. What works wonderfully and efficiently for one individual could have little or no affect on another. Balance is relative according to one's truth. This phenomenon reveals the Law of Ma'at in operation.

* * *

Some days later, Ananya was spending time in the city. She felt led to reconnect with some friends, a lovely couple who owned a yoga/spiritual center. When Ananya told them what had been occurring and her decision to commit to a life of sharing her knowledge, they invited her to give an impromptu talk at their center that weekend. Although she felt unsure of herself, she agreed to do it; she needed to get her feet wet. The fact that this opportunity presented itself so soon was surely a sign that All That Is fully supported her decision.

On the day of the talk, 10 people showed up—a good number for feet-wetting. Feeling nervous, Ananya spoke a bit about the Divine Laws of Healing, then invited questions and discussion.

A woman in the group pointed out that Ananya looked "awfully young" and questioned what authority she had.

Flustered, Ananya recognized that she had just outwardly manifested her inner doubts—and now had to deal with them. "*This is my test,*" she thought.

She took a deep breath. "*Ma'am, I feel age is totally irrelevant. In fact, small children are probably the truest sages of our time. I am simply sharing my truth, and I fully respect that it may not be your truth. In fact, don't believe a single word I say. Instead, receive my words and measure them against your own truth and guidance: Only you can know what is true for you. I invite you to discern truth in your hearts. Go away with that which resonates with you and leave behind that which does not. Albert Einstein said, 'All knowledge of reality starts in experience and ends in it.' I encourage you to observe the experience you have with these Divine Laws, and then draw your own conclusions.*"

This response calmed the accusing woman and Ananya went on to lead a lively interactive discussion—one that everyone enjoyed.

* * *

That night, Ananya had a dream about Ma'at. In her dream, they were sitting together atop a cloud having a conversation.

"*You lived my Law tonight.*"

"*I believe I lived the counter aspect of your Law tonight.*"

"*Indeed. You were shown a negative aspect of this Law to gain a better understanding of how the positive aspect operates. The Law of Ma'at is about balance within one's being. The woman who judged you was very imbalanced in her being; her judgment had nothing to do with you at all."*

"I know you're right, but it's unpleasant knowing that I will meet adversaries if I come out with my truth."

"There are and will continue to be 'adversaries'. . . . they too are a part of All That Is. In fact, 'adversaries' or 'unknowingness', as I prefer to call it, is actually part of the healing process."

"How is that, Ma'at?"

"This is a planet of choice and free will. Individuals can choose the easy way to learn, or they can choose the difficult way. If someone chooses to have difficulties, it simply means choosing the path of 'unknowing' rather than the path of 'knowing.' One is a path of light— knowing who one BE in All That Is; One is a path of darkness—which is simply 'unknowingness'. On this path of darkness, one eventually realizes who one is NOT. Realizing who one is NOT leads to understanding who one IS. Same thing, just a different way of going about it, do you see?"

Ananya smiled at this completely non-judgmental and unconditionally loving way of viewing existence.

"Many see the forces of darkness as the greatest adversary of all, and in the world of appearances, that may be so. However, in going beyond the world of appearances and illusions to complete the whole energy, the 'adversary' actually performs a service for the greater good. The word 'adversary' in itself is a judgment because it

implies a separation between 'us' and 'them.' That is an illusion. It is important to recognize that those whom you refer to as adversary—or even those you refer to as 'evil'—are also a part of All That Is, just as much as you and I are. The point is balance—to accept both the light and the shadow within one's self because these two aspects are balance. And balance is crucial to healing, of any kind."

Ananya lay her head down in Ma'at's lap and rested peacefully. The next morning, she awoke and remembered her dream as if it had been real; as if she had actually been sitting atop a cloud, conversing with a Goddess.

9

The Law of Elements

ANANYA RENTED A CAR and drove south into the stunning alpine wilderness of New Zealand's south island. Throughout her travels, she had often found herself in the midst of spectacular landscape such as this, but this place *felt* different somehow.

At the edge of a turquoise-colored lake surrounded by snow-capped mountains, she found a vacant lodge and didn't see a reason to drive farther. Ananya spent several days in this heavenly area, exploring her surroundings by foot. At the end of one such day, she sat at the edge of the lake and watched the reflection of the peaks on the water's surface.

Then, just like that, she felt the humming vibration around her heart. It gave her a sense of both comfort and excitement, for she knew it meant that it was time to move on to the next Law. The voice she heard was very deep—it seemed to come up from the depths of the lake.

"The 9th Universal Law is the Law of Transformation. All That Is is in a constant state of movement, a constant state of transformation. The Buddha taught about the permanent state of impermanence in the universe. The Buddha was referring to the Universal Law of Transformation. Even the balance that one finds in Law #8 is impermanent. When one is standing still, one is in that state of equilibrium. However, in order to move, one has to lift one foot slightly off the ground to take a step forward, thus temporarily losing equilibrium. Once the step forward is complete, another state of equilibrium is established . . . and yet one would find himself in a different place than he was before, would he not?"

"Yes."

"There is another possibility. The individual could remain standing still and never take a step, although it might make certain things rather difficult indeed."

"Cute sense of humor," she thought.

"Thank you. You are cute too, little one. However, it is true that this 9th Law is where many in your world get stuck every day, like a bug in the spider's web. Unable to move forward, they get eaten up in a certain sense of the term. That is why the 9th Law of Healing is required to assist one in breaking free from that sticky web, if one so chooses. As always, we walk beside you."

* * *

Ananya continued driving southwest, passing mile after mile of unadulterated land until she reached Mt.

Aspiring National Park. While driving, her thoughts turned to a bothersome email she'd received from a colleague of hers. The colleague informed her that because she had been away so long and hadn't handed in any stories, her editor was engaging another writer. It looked like this person might take Ananya's place permanently. She agreed that this was a reasonable action, and she *had* decided to leave her job anyway. *"I really shouldn't have any problem with this,"* she rationalized, and yet she struggled with some feelings of resentment. *"My editor doesn't know about my decision,"* she mulled. *"Doesn't he value me enough after all these years to wait for my return home next week?"* These thoughts tumbled around in her head, giving her a headache.

She parked the car to explore this vast national park on foot and came across a pristine, turquoise-colored river. *"What a delight for the eyes as well as the spirit,"* she thought as she sat beside the river and watched the water. Ever since she was a child, water had always fascinated her. She could sit for hours by a brook just watching the way it flowed. Her observation of water had taught her many things.

Water is a metaphor for spirit. The way water flows down a river symbolizes the way the human spirit begins from one source and journeys through life. Sometimes the waters are calm; sometimes they are rough. But no matter the conditions, water doesn't stop flowing. Eventually, it meets with its source again.

Water is also a master of illusion. By looking at its surface one can't even comprehend the mysteries that lay beneath. Water covers unknown magic and therefore commands respect.

As Ananya connected with the energy of water now, she momentarily felt herself *become* the water. She felt the call of respect it commanded, not in a dictatorial way, but in a loving, nurturing way. After all, water is our nourishment, our life. And certainly that life calls for respect.

At that moment, Ananya connected so deeply with the water that she could no longer separate herself from it or any of the four other elements. Fire, earth, wood, and air all dwelt equally within her.

She took a deep breath of air. As she exhaled, it felt like an exchange of love between her and All That Is. At that moment she realized that every breath, whether conscious or unconscious, is the continuous exchange of love that flows between humans, plants, animals . . . it is *All That Is* loving *All That Is.*

Ananya then understood why she sensed a different energy here than other places of great beauty. In New Zealand the five elements were in harmony with one another. She felt waves of energy running through her body again and was then able to remember that the Law of Elements is the 9th Law of Healing, addressing the Universal Law of Transformation. This Law shows that *respect* for the elements within us and about us is the bridge to graceful transformation.

All That Is is indeed in a constant state of motion, a constant state of transformation. But unless we respect that motion, and allow the movement to occur gracefully, it can get blocked, causing great dis-ease.

How did this Law apply in her own situation? Her ego was experiencing resentment that her place at work had been taken so quickly, even though, in reality, it was the best possible thing for all concerned.

Resentment is that "sticky" energy the great beings had referred to, she realized. Unless she could view her work situation with divine respect, it would be a challenge for her to gracefully move on with her life. Ananya acknowledged that she had actually created this situation; her own soul had called it forth with her decision to follow her truth. *"So how could I not have respect for the magnificent creation of my soul?"* she asked herself. Seeing the situation from that perspective allowed her energy to shift completely and open both her mind and her heart, more fully to her future.

* * *

After spending a good deal of time processing and integrating the Law of Elements into her own life, she left the breathtaking national park to find a place to eat. Once seated at a local café, Ananya took out her notebook—which was looking very 'well-traveled' by now—and a pen and wrote whatever came. . . .

Because emotion is simply energy in motion, it's important to respect and allow that energy to move. Consider an individual who's feeling anger, for example. This is natural; after all, anger is a human emotion and we are here to experience being human. But anger wants to move, as all energy does. Given the chance, it can move out of the body as quickly as it enters into it. Having respect for one's self and the emotion they are experiencing facilitates that movement.

But instead of respect, many people judge themselves for feeling a certain way—"Oh, well, I shouldn't be feeling anger so I'll pretend I'm not feeling it." A judgment like that stops the motion of anger dead in its tracks. When emotion is not allowed to move in a natural, healthy way, it moves in an unhealthy way. It eventually manifests itself in physical form, causing dis-ease within the individual.

Applying that concept, Ananya understood that her headache had been the result of her resistance to the Law of Elements. The energy of disrespect, especially in the form of self-criticism, causes one's head to ache.

The Law of Creation states that everything is within. Applying that here means that nobody can make another feel an emotion that is not *already present* within them. In fact, whoever or whatever triggers the emotion—whether it is anger, jealousy, hatred, etc.—is helping the person move through it. And the best way to move through an emotion is to allow oneself to feel it fully—it is part of embracing the shadow, that one may then be able to embrace one's light.

* * *

The few weeks Ananya spent in New Zealand had been extremely nourishing, but the time had come to return home and deal with all the changes—both internally and externally. She still had three more laws to rediscover, but since she fully realized the Laws lived *within* her, she knew that it really didn't matter where she was—sitting in her own home, she would remember the next Law.

10

The Law of Welcome

BEING BACK IN THE UNITED STATES proved even more of an adjustment than Ananya had anticipated. Not only was she without her job, but even the place didn't feel right to her anymore. She couldn't relate to certain friends and even her own apartment no longer felt like home. Ananya's frequency had shifted so much that the energy she previously associated with no longer resonated with her. She felt like a fish out of water, exhausted all the time, with little motivation to do anything at all.

She sat on her couch and looked around at all her things. A few months ago, they would have conjured feelings of security. But now, she barely recognized her belongings. Frightened, she realized all her security was gone. She *felt* as if she had lost everything, though she actually hadn't.

Struggling to BE in this situation, Ananya knew she had come far, progressing through nine dimensions of love. Now it was time to enter the dimension of "love in action"—yet inertia ruled her life.

As she lay in her bed one morning, she recalled her dream about the Pyramids of Giza, and the first time the great beings had communicated with her. How magical it had all been! At this moment, she wished to go back to that magical time. She decided to call on them and within a few moments a voice—this time with an elderly, grandfatherly quality to it—resounded in her head.

"*The 10th Law of the Universe is the Law of Release. Emptiness is a prerequisite to fullness. Unless you are willing to be empty, you have no space to be filled up. At the moment you are having some resistance to this Law. That is not a criticism; in fact, it is appropriate because through your resistance, you gain a more complete understanding of just how the 10th Law of Healing operates.*"

"Why do I feel so exhausted all the time?"

"*You find yourself in an energy that makes you uncomfortable because you feel you are beyond it now, and you are. However, just because you have moved beyond the energy of this place does not mean that you cannot still embrace it for what it is. You are fighting with this energy instead of embracing it. Though the energy does not resonate with you anymore, it is still a part of All That Is. It is possible to remain detached from the energy while embracing it at the same time. It is called being in the world, but not of the world. Sound familiar?*"

Waves of energy began running through Ananya's body again—as if her "pipeline" connected to this Law had just been unclogged. She instantly remembered that the Law of Welcome is the 10th Law of Healing, addressing the Universal Law of Release. The Law of Welcome is about wholeheartedly embracing All That Is, and *whatever* All That Is has to offer. With the application of this 10th Divine Law of Healing, a life of struggle becomes a life of ease and grace.

"Thank you . . . I needed that!"

"It is our pleasure. As always, we walk beside you."

As she had always done, Ananya proceeded to write down whatever sprung forth from within.

Whatever our soul calls forth in our life is always exactly what we need at exactly the right time. However, blessings come in a variety of forms. Many of these forms do not resemble blessings at all. Sometimes the form is a door that closes on an opportunity, or a heart-wrenching break-up, or even the death of a child. Sometimes the form is an open door to an opportunity, the love of a lifetime or the birth of a child. No matter what it is or in what form it comes, if we have the courage to welcome and embrace it wholeheartedly, we can feel and know our intimate connection with All That Is.

When we are not embracing what is, however it is, we are attempting to control what is. That's when we feel disconnected from not only everything and everyone around us, but from ourselves as well. Whatever challenges one may be facing in life, no matter how big, they are perfectly appropriate and timely for one's journey into the heart of

All That Is. Therefore, they should be embraced as gifts, not as curses.

* * *

Feeling totally revitalized, Ananya got the sudden urge to go for a run on the beach. Her tiredness disappeared the moment she applied the Law of Welcome and embraced wholeheartedly everything around her—including the place that she didn't belong to anymore.

Running barefoot on the sand, Ananya thought, *"Just as nature recreates itself at every moment, it also embraces All That Is at every moment. The ocean waves come crashing onto the beach, and yet the sand doesn't stand up and reject the force of the waves. Instead, it embraces each wave and then gracefully lets it go, trusting that the next wave is on its way. This is what living in bliss is all about."* She realized that the Law of Welcome is the open door—the gateway into the heart of All That Is,—just as the shadow is the gateway to the light. When one embraces the shadow wholeheartedly, one invites in true joy and light into one's life.

Deep in contemplation, Ananya didn't see a fishing line planted in the beach. She ran right into it, getting slightly tangled. She heard someone with an Irish accent ask, "Are you alright?" And out of the corner of her eye, she caught sight of a tall man walking towards her.

"Oh, I'm fine . . . ," she said as she untangled herself. *"I'm sorry about your fishing line . . . I was. . . . "*

Then she looked up at him and their eyes met.

"You look familiar," she said.

"Yeah," he agreed, "You look familiar too . . . hi, my name is Zachary."

"I'm Ananya," she reached her hand out to touch his.

"That's a beautiful name, 'Ananya' . . . . I believe it means 'unique' in Sanskrit?"

Impressed, Ananya acknowledged that he was correct. They chatted about where they could have possibly seen each other before. Interestingly, they talked as if they had known each other for years.

Zachary invited this woman who'd interrupted his fishing to have a seat with him on the beach. Ananya laughed at his wonderful sense of humor. Zachary was mesmerized by her big green eyes and profoundly attracted to her light. He couldn't explain how, but he knew that he loved this woman long before he ever met her. He'd been waiting patiently for her to walk into his life—just like he'd been waiting patiently for the fish to bite his line.

The thought flashed through Ananya's mind that her entire life had led her to this beach at this moment. And this place of South Florida that she no longer resonated with held a precious gift that had been waiting for her to embrace. Though this appeared to have been some freak, chance meeting, she knew she'd found *him*, the soul that she'd agreed to unite with in this life, before she even came into this life. She also couldn't explain how she knew; she just knew. And that produced both feelings of intense joy, but also intense fear; she had been alone for so long that she wasn't even sure of how to handle a person being in her life. In a split second, she decided to accept and embrace both these feelings and throw herself into what was happening.

The two spent the following weeks together, falling deeper and deeper in love. It was time to dream another dream, for both of them—one that was about unity on all levels. It didn't take long for Zachary to propose marriage. When Ananya said yes, they both felt that they trusted themselves and one another enough to allow their marriage to take place right away. Ananya and Zachary married within a couple of months, holding a multicultural ceremony in front of family and close friends.

Ananya felt so grateful that she'd decided to embrace All That Is, and whatever All That Is had to offer her. By doing so, she was finally able to accept the precious gift that All That Is had for her—her life companion.

Soon after the wedding, the two left to celebrate their union in beautiful Costa Rica. Soul and Spirit were now united in blissful matrimony and it was indeed great cause for celebration.

11

The Law of Gratitude

Some believe that Costa Rica is located at the "heart chakra" of the earth. In a similar way that human beings have chakras (energy centers) and meridians (energy pathways), so does Mother Earth. And if Costa Rica is indeed located at the heart chakra of earth, the energy of that place would be very healing.

The newlyweds arrived at the San Jose airport, rented a car, and began a four-hour drive to Arenal, in the center of this small Central American country. As they drove, they both felt an unmistakable "aliveness" about the place—as if every tree, bird, and gushing waterfall had their hearts open to life.

When they arrived, the Arenal volcano greeted them with a puff of smoke. It is an active volcano and this display reminded them of a great queen sitting majestically atop her throne, blowing kisses toward her subjects. They stopped at a beautiful private lodge located at the foot of the queen herself.

* * *

Zachary and Ananya sat late into the night watching the volcano spew lava down her broad body. Every once in a while, the queen would breathe; it sounded like an "ohm" coming from the very core of the earth. When the volcano breathed, Zach and Ananya took a deep breath also. And in the sharing of the breath, they felt intimately connected with the volcano, with one another, and with everything else that was breathing. It was as if all of creation at that moment just took one deep breath and the exhale was a mantra of gratitude to God.

This time, without the assistance of her celestial friends, her deep experience of the 11th Law of the Universe sparked the knowing of it within her. Because she knew the Laws of Healing were within her, it meant the Laws of the Universe were also within her. The 11th Universal Law is the Law of Connection, the last of the four primary laws, which means that nothing in All That Is is disconnected; everything is intimately connected.

After the Universal Law of Release created an empty space, one can experience the Universal Law of Connection—feeling the utter fullness of being connected to All That Is.

Ananya called on the great beings to thank them for their loving guidance and presence with her always. And, of course, they were already there. Zachary, being a highly sensitive man, could actually see all of them. They appeared to him like huge columns of light standing side by side.

Ananya was amazed at this because even she had never actually seen all of them. *"How many do you see?"* she asked Zach.

He counted 13 of them. Their presence always brought a feeling of ecstasy that was hard to describe. Zachary hadn't been able to comprehend Ananya's attempts at explaining this feeling until he experienced it for himself.

Ananya had usually communicated telepathically with these great beings, but this time she spoke to them out loud for Zach's benefit.

"I'm sure you can read my heart, but I want to thank you for choosing me and for always walking beside me."

"We thank you for the opportunity you have given us. We have not chosen you; you have chosen us. We had been waiting and hoping to do this work with you, and it has been a tremendous joy for us. You must understand that the joy you feel now feeds us, and we thank you for that."

She bowed her head with her palms together at the heart. She was so filled with gratitude, for everything, and everyone—even for those who had caused her pain in the past, for they had contributed to her being who she is today. With tears of joy in her eyes she said *"There is nothing more fulfilling than just being the spoke that I AM in the wheel of All That Is."*

She recalled that the 11th Divine Law of Healing is the Law of Gratitude. The Law of Gratitude addresses the

Universal Law of Connection because it is through gratitude for All That Is, that we understand our connection to
All That Is.

The 13 beings continued to speak in one voice.

*"We have pointed out that each law addresses a par-
ticular frequency of love. Laws 9, 10, and 11 can be called
'love in action.' Once one aligns to the first eight frequencies of love, then it's possible to understand that one is love
itself. And with that understanding, one becomes love in
action. So one shows respect for All That Is, then wel-
comes what All That Is has to offer, and then gives
thanks for it.*

*It is important to remember that these Laws do oper-
ate simultaneously, and so separating one Law from the
others can in fact become a limitation, a chore that one has
to do, rather than a means of expanding one's BEing. So,
for example, respect without gratitude becomes 'I have to
respect—or else.' It lacks warmth. It becomes a condition. Any action that begins with the thought 'I have to' in-
dicates a conditional energy, as opposed to an
unconditional energy that is without limitation. So, the
outcome of an action conditioned by 'I have to' will be
limited."*

"That is very powerful."

*"The Laws of love in action are very powerful,
indeed, and cannot be 'impeded' without cost. In place of
respect there is resentment. In place of welcome, there is
rejection and exclusion. In place of gratitude, there is
blame."*

"I see." Ananya recognized how we often blame instead of feel gratitude for those who have taught us the tough but valuable lessons in life.

"Now it's time for us to leave you two to your celebration. As always, we walk beside you."

"Wow!" Zachary remarked. "I could actually feel them leave and yet I still feel their energy around us."

"They are still around us," she said, *"And in us."* Ananya somehow knew this to be true.

Dawn was breaking. The birds sang their morning ragas; dewdrops decorated the grass; and the volcano went into hiding behind thick cloud.

"We stayed up the whole night. How are you feeling, sweetie?" Ananya asked while yawning.

"Actually, I feel completely charged," Zachary said. "Like every cell in my body is jumping up and down for joy . . . it's crazy, but I feel like dancing!" Then he went outside and began dancing with reckless abandon on the grass, in the midst of grazing horses. Zach's child-like enthusiasm brought Ananya great joy. She knew his dance emerged from the purity and innocence of his heart—what is meant by the biblical phrase "Be ye like children." She joined him in this beautiful expression of joy and gratitude.

They laughed and danced together to an audience of horses, and then skipped back into their room, fell onto the bed, and made passionate love till noon.

* * *

Zachary and Ananya eventually left Costa Rica with the sense that they would return, perhaps even to settle down there. But with only the 12th Law left to remember, Ananya wished to return to Egypt now—the place where she began this incredible journey.

12

The Infinite Wave

BACK IN GIZA AT THE PYRAMIDS, Ananya had come full circle, and not just geographically. She led her husband to the same spot where she had sat six months before and had her first interaction with the great beings. As they sat together quietly, Ananya felt that yet another journey was about to commence; only this one would be on a whole new level. This time, she would journey in union with her beloved.

They spent a long time in reverent silence in front of the Pyramids of Giza until it seemed like they had *become* the Pyramids—just as Ananya had become one with the water before. They felt no separation between anything or anyone . . . all *is* ONE.

As Ananya experienced this ONE-ness, she realized that All That Is is only vibrations, and that these vibrations move at different speeds on different frequencies. It is their movement which identifies the vibration as either the color blue, the smell of a rose, or a hard surface, and so on.

It's the *movement* of these vibrations that creates the grand and glorious symphony of All That Is. And in the midst of this symphony exists nothing—the no-thing-ness. And nothingness is the seed of all potentiality. Everything there IS is birthed out of nothing.

The wave of All That Is is constantly moving. Everything comes from nothing and moves back into nothing, which then is everything again! All That Is operates as an Infinite Wave.

At that moment, her body absolutely buzzing with energy, Ananya remembered the 12th Divine Law of Healing, simply called The Infinite Wave. This time, without any humming sensation around her heart, Ananya heard the familiar voices speaking in the form of thoughts in her head.

"You are feeling at ONE with All That Is."

"Yes. Yes, I am."

"The 12th Law of the Universe is called At-One-Ment. All is ONE in the heart of All That Is; the appearance of any separation within All That Is is an illusion. All That Is is truly one being, expressing itself in a variety of ways."

Ananya listened in ecstasy, being aware of herself and yet, at the same time, feeling she was no longer herself. She recognized that the great beings who spoke with her were not outside of her at all. *They were her and she was them.* She now understood what Jesus meant when he said, "I and the Father are one."

The voices continued, *"Humanity once knew and lived At-One-Ment, until feelings of guilt took over the consciousness."*

"What has mankind felt guilty for?"

"For forgetting who they truly BE, and for crucifying themselves. This is eloquently portrayed by the crucifixion of Christ, a most significant symbol indeed, because it represents humanity's denial of the shadow. Jesus Christ, by simply BEing, sought to facilitate souls in acknowledging and embracing their shadow so that they may live more fully in their light. The Christ himself represents the shadow of mankind."

Ananya recalled the 3rd Law of Healing, the Law of Completion, which addresses the Universal Law of Duality and Frequency. That Law states that the shadow is not the "dark side," but simply the hidden aspect, the other half of the yin/yang, the *counterpoint to be whole.*

The voices continued, *"When the Christ proclaimed: 'I am the way, the truth and the life; no man cometh unto the Father but by me' (John 14:6), he was saying, 'No one comes to the light but by the shadow.' Together, Father and Son, Light and Shadow, signify wholeness of being. However, instead of embracing the wholeness of who they BE, mankind inwardly denied the shadow part of their being, and outwardly denied "the son" and crucified him. Denial causes separation, and a feeling of separation turns At-One-Ment into atonement.*

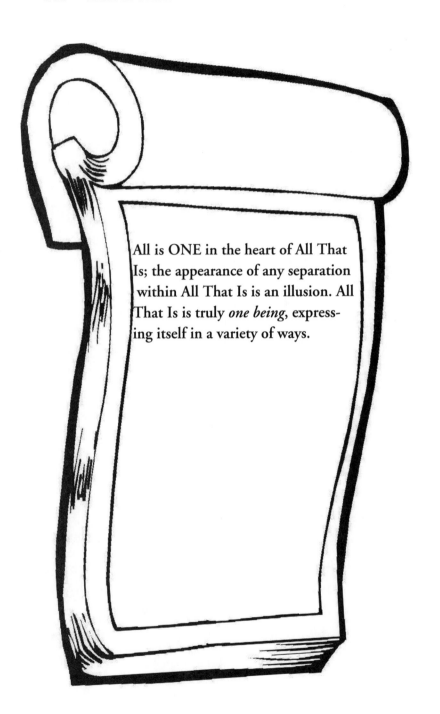

All is ONE in the heart of All That Is; the appearance of any separation within All That Is is an illusion. All That Is is truly *one being*, expressing itself in a variety of ways.

Our message to humanity is: You are Love-pure and innocent. It is time to be set free from the illusion of guilt. Because where there is no illusion, there is no dis-ease of any kind."

Tears flowed down Ananya's face as she looked over at her beloved Zach, deep in meditation. *"What a thin line between atonement and At-One-Ment!"* she thought. In written form, it was the mere difference of two hyphens. But in life, the difference between atonement and At-One-Ment was the shift of an entire paradigm of reality.

"So, I have remembered all 12 Divine Laws of Healing and now the journey is complete."

"Well, you know, the journey is not over. The journey is never over. It only progresses to higher and higher levels of BEing. By living the 12 Laws in your own way, you have completed one cycle of the 12 dimensions of BEing, and in this process, you have progressed from the outer of All That Is to the inner of All That Is. Once you reach the innermost heart of All That Is, you go back out again to start over—but on a higher level. To this circular progression, there is no end."

"I am seeing a never-ending spiral of energy, expanding limitlessly outward in all directions. That spiral is the Infinite Wave of All That Is! Is that true?"

"That is it exactly. Every thought, feeling, and action in All That Is follows the principles inherent in this symbol of the spiral. All energy in All That Is flows in a progressive circular pattern, creating spiral on top of spiral, which has no limits and no end."

A main purpose of the human mind is to define and decipher the *limitations* of reality. And Ananya acknowledged that to grasp the concept of utter limitlessness was not for the mind, but for the heart and soul.

From Outer to Inner

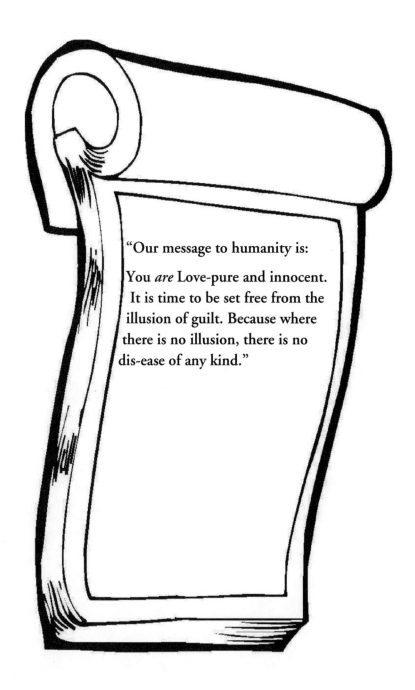

"Our message to humanity is:

You *are* Love–pure and innocent. It is time to be set free from the illusion of guilt. Because where there is no illusion, there is no dis-ease of any kind."

The voices continued, "Once one has progressed from outer to inner, the return back to outer needs to have the energy of sharing. That is why we implore you to share your knowledge, your experiences, and most importantly, your heart—unconditionally—with others."

Ananya would do this, not by *doing*, but simply by *being* who she is. The great beings had once told her that by the end of her journey, she would understand this profundity, and she did. From *being* who she is, the *doing* would arise—naturally, as it should. She would write a book, which would present the opportunity for its readers to remember, acknowledge, and step into the truth of who *they* BE.

* * *

Zachary opened his eyes and reached out for his wife's hand. Although he had been having his own individual experience, it had not been separate from hers. The camel drivers started to become a nuisance, so they got up, brushed the sand off their legs, and headed toward the Sphinx, the guardian of these 12 "houses" of universal knowledge and wisdom.

The outwardly expanding spiral of the Laws

The KEY

SEATED ATOP A BLOCK OF ANCIENT STONE, Ananya recapped the 12 Divine Laws of Healing with Zach, who jotted down what each Law's quintessential point is.

The **Law of Creation** states that all of creation is within us, and so we create and recreate who we BE, and how we experience that BEing, at every moment.

The **Law of Love** states that unconditional love is the true essence of every single living creature—we need only be vulnerable enough to allow that *unconditional love* to flow.

The **Law of Completion** states that through completion—a commitment to go beyond the appearances of reality, to see the significance of what truly *is*—we understand the divine duality of All That Is.

The Law of Manifestation states that "As above, so below." Energy manifests as matter; recreate the energy, recreate the manifestation of matter, and thus, recreate attraction.

The Law of Evolution states that All That Is is in a continuous cycle of birth and death and rebirth.

The Law of Free Will states that each individual is free to will anything and everything in the ever-abundant universe.

The Law of Equality states that all in All That Is is equal. Each on his or her own appropriate path, none is superior to another.

The Law of Ma'at (Balance) states that All That Is seeks to maintain balance. Truth and justice are the keys to balance, and balance is the key to choice.

The Law of Elements states that a respect for All That Is is required for transformation in All That Is.

The Law of Welcome states that by embracing All That Is, and whatever All That Is has to offer, we release our struggle and open ourselves to the heart of All That Is.

The Law of Gratitude states that gratitude for All That Is is the key to feeling and knowing our intimate connection with All That Is.

The Infinite Wave states that All That Is is made of vibrations—moving in one wave, *as one being*.

Ananya knew that there was so much more to these Divine Laws than she could fully comprehend yet; the Laws are dynamic living energies, so they too, are constantly moving, shifting, and changing. She was confident that an even deeper understanding of the Laws of Healing would grow with time and experience.

With one last mystery to solve, the couple slowly returned up the hill toward the smallest of the three main pyramids, the one referred to as the Pyramid of Mycerinus.

"I am sure that is the Pyramid that doesn't house a Law," Ananya told Zach. *"The 13th one, as it were"*

"Have you figured out what it represents?"

"I have a feeling it has something to do with accessing the 12 Laws."

Stopping a distance from the Pyramid and the crowds, Ananya addressed the ones who walked beside her.

"What about the 13th Pyramid?" she asked them. *"What does it represent?"*

On one side of the Pyramid, she was shown the image of an ancient holy book that possessed a lock. In old times, she had learned, sacred books were normally bound with locks. The only way to access them was to unlock them with a . . . key. That was it! The 13th Pyramid represents the key to unlocking all the wisdom and knowledge of the universe.

"But what is that key and who holds it?" she asked.

"Why don't you tell us what the key is and who holds it, keeper of the Divine Laws of Healing?"

Ananya placed her hands on her heart and allowed the answer to surface. It arose as a feeling, which she attempted to translate into words.

"Every human being on the planet holds this key within his or her own heart. As one unlocks one's heart, one unlocks the heart of All That Is, because the heart of All That Is is within. So, the key, simply, is to BE. To access all the wisdom and knowledge of the universe, we need only to access our self."

"*Indeed.*"

"One more question: You reminded me that I'm a custodian, a keeper of the Divine Laws of Healing. Surely I'm not the only keeper of these Divine Laws . . . not the only one capable of sharing their wisdom?"

"*It is true; you are not the only one. There are seven custodians all together. However, only three of you are actually incarnated into a physical body at this time. And the other two, besides you, will offer their own perspective on the Laws of Healing, and that is entirely appropriate. And there are others too, who are not custodians of these Laws, but who are aware of their connection to them. They, too, will offer their ideas. These Laws are vast in their totality, requiring diverse perspectives. And each perspective is significant because, when integrated together, they will lead to a fuller understanding of existence—on all frequencies.*"

"That sounds right to me! I have another question."

"*Yes, little one. Please ask many questions, always.*"

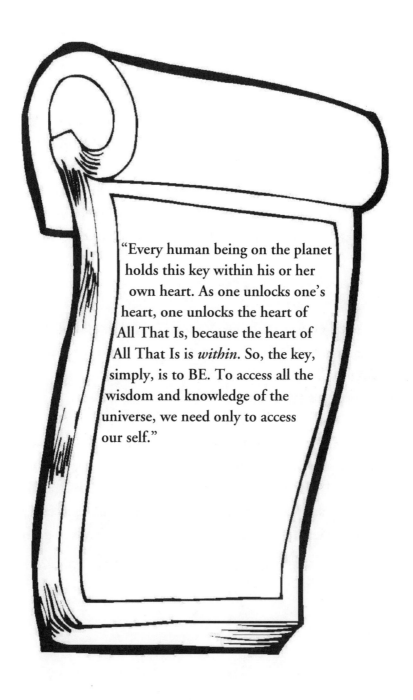

"Every human being on the planet holds this key within his or her own heart. As one unlocks one's heart, one unlocks the heart of All That Is, because the heart of All That Is is *within*. So, the key, simply, is to BE. To access all the wisdom and knowledge of the universe, we need only to access our self."

"I have seen you outside of me, and I feel you inside of me at the same time. I have felt that you are me. Would you please explain . . . who you are, exactly?"

"We like to call ourselves the Infinite Stars of Light. We are the various aspects of All That Is. We are all the elements of nature. We are the Pyramids. We are the aspects of you, just as you are an expression of us in the world. We are all the Laws, and, as you know, the Laws are not something outside of you, they are within you . . . they are you. Just like we are you and you are us . . . all is one."

"Zachary counted 13 of you when he saw you in Costa Rica."

"Yes, he saw us quite clearly. Isn't it interesting that every major world paradigm manifests a master plus 12 disciples?"

Ananya's jaw dropped. *"You mean . . . "*

Just then, she understood—she was part of the dawning of a new world paradigm—one in which we all step back into BEing and embrace the unity of All That Is. One in which we let go of atonement and remember At-One-Ment. One in which we let go of perceived guilt and are, once again, free to BE . . . *innocent.*

Enlightenment is synonymous with freedom, which is recognizing that there is nothing to do, nowhere to go, and no one to become. It is about BEing who you are, however you are, in each moment . . . and *that* is innocence.

12 Universal Laws		12 Laws of Healing
Law of Being	1	Law of Creation
Law of Love	2	Law of Love
Law of Duality/Frequency	3	Law of Completion
Law of Attraction	4	Law of Manifestation
Law of Contrast	5	Law of Evolution
Law of Abundance	6	Law of Free Will
Law of Limitations	7	Law of Equality
Law of Choice	8	Law of Ma'at (Balance)
Law of Transformation	9	Law of Elements
Law of Release	10	Law of Welcome
Law of Connection	11	Law of Gratitude
At-One-Ment	12	The Infinite Wave

ABOUT THE AUTHOR

Born in 1970 to Indian and Turkish parents, Lara A. Shah is truly a global citizen. After obtaining an undergraduate degree in Political Science and Anthropology from Japan, Lara went on to attend Graduate school in Turkey, pursuing a Masters degree in Sociology. She worked as an International Business Analyst in Asia, and then a Journalist covering Eastern Europe and Central Asia for various prestigious news publications. In her early 30's, Lara's life turned upside down causing her to remember who she truly BE and to reconnect with her God-given gift to facilitate others in profound healing on all levels. Then, in 2002, a near-death experience high in the Andes of Peru catalyzed Lara's commitment to serve humanity with her powerful gift. Initiated as a Shaman, Lara founded and developed "The KEY", a self-empowering healing process based on the 12 Divine Laws of Healing. Today, Lara has an international practice spanning three continents. She continuously tours the world holding private and group healing sessions, teaching classes and holding workshops to facilitate higher consciousness.

To learn more about Lara's work, visit her website at:
www.lawsofhealing.com
Personal correspondence may be addressed to:
lara@lawsofhealing.com

To book Lara A. Shah for a teaching/speaking event anywhere in the world, please contact:

Aquarian Age Publishing, Inc.
102 NE 2nd Street #141
Boca Raton, FL 33432 U.S.A
Telephone: (1) 561 329 3417
Email: author@aquarianagepublishing.com

Aquarian Age Publishing, Inc.

"The Age of Aquarius is the age when human beings will arise in spiritual light; when men and women will learn to use the full power of the soul"

"The Light Bringer–The Ray of John and the Age of Intuition" By: White Eagle
The White Eagle Publishing Trust 2001

Aquarian Age Publishing, Inc. was formed with the purpose of offering books—both fiction and non-fiction—CDs, children's educational materials, and other such resources, that present and promote universal wisdom in an easy and entertaining manner.

To order more copies of this book, please visit www.aquarianagepublishing.com

The following discounts are offered on bulk purchases:

Quantity of Order	Percent of Discount
5–19 copies	10%
20–99 copies	20%
100 and up	40%